C000269451

Hive Magic

Other Series by Sarah K. L. Wilson

Dragon School

Dragon Chameleon

Dragon Tide

Bridge of Legends

Tangled Fae

Empire of War & Wings
Book 2

Sarah K. L. Wilson

Published by Sarah K. L. Wilson, 2020

This is a work of fiction. Similarities to real people, places, or events are entirely coincidental.
HIVE MAGIC
First Edition. September 15, 2020

ISBN : 978-1-7772645-1-2
Cover Art by Luciano Fleitas
Written by Sarah K. L. Wilson
www.sarahklwilson.com

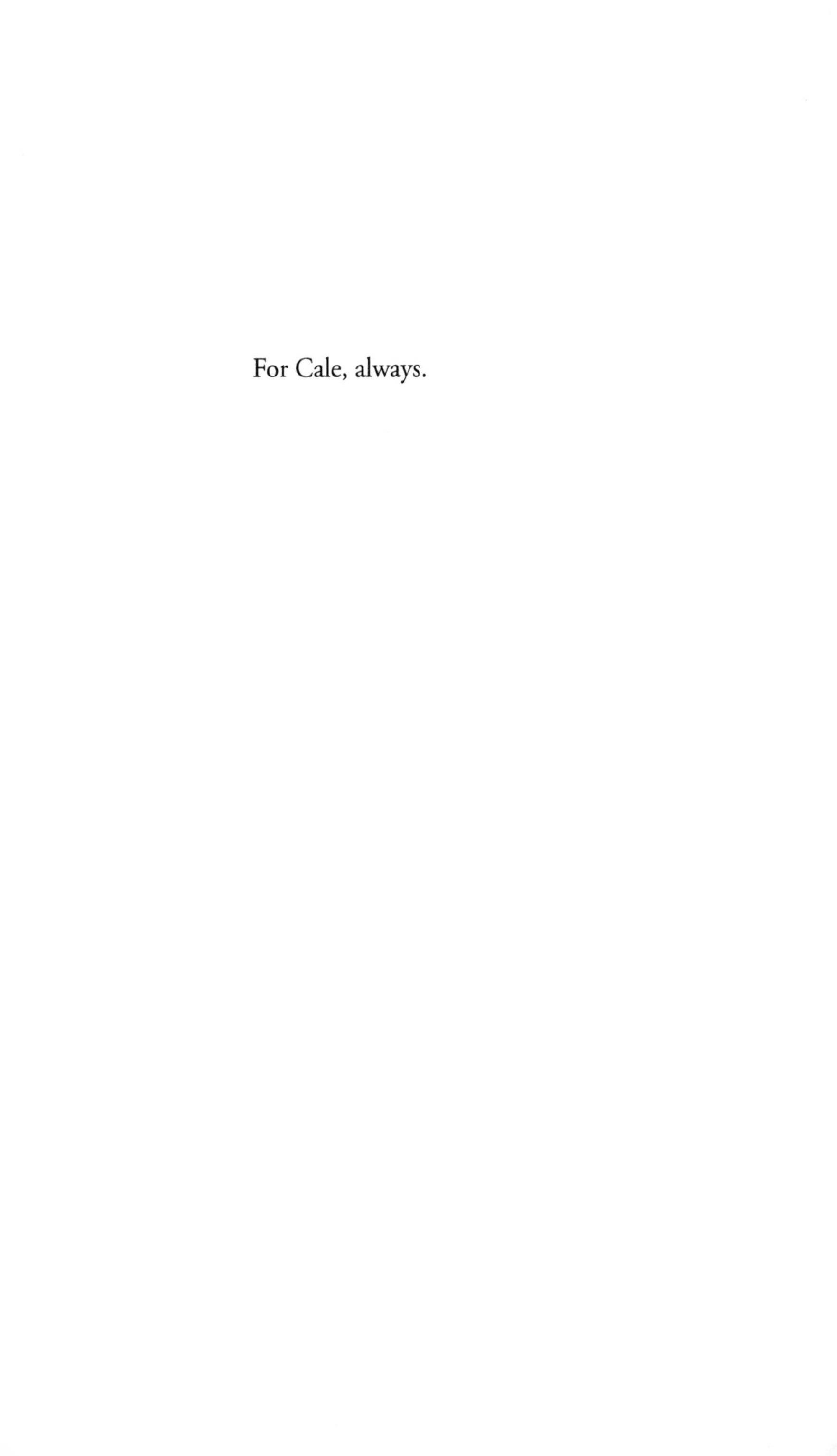

For Cale, always.

PREVIOUSLY IN THE WINGED EMPIRE

The crown prince took all the weapons from the people of Far Stones and they had no way to defend themselves from the dark magic that lurks there.

Aella was meant to Hatch into someone who manifests a magic bird but she Hatched bees instead.

The crown prince says he owns her now, and she's afraid to defy him in case he takes it out on her family like the way he killed her father.

Her allies are Zayana, Osprey, and Ivo.

But Osprey is linked to the crown prince through magic and he's bound to stop any moves made against the throne.

Ivo wants her to be part of a secret revolution – a revolution that he and Osprey have already committed to.

But everything changed when the prince manifested snakes in an underground cathedral.

And that's what you need to know.

BOOK ONE: OUT OF THE HIVE

On the cusp of the zephyr,

The edge of the breeze,

On the peak of the hurricane,

We find our ease.

Dance with the torrent,

Drift over the tide,

Embrace the tornado,

But live for the ride.

Songs of the Winged Ones

Elsewhere in the Winged Empire

He was seeing things. That was the only reasonable explanation.

Trassel Isle was the most boring post in the Winged Empire and any Claw sent here was either close to retirement – like he was – or too thick in the head to manage harder duties. He didn't mind the quiet most of the time, but tonight, something had felt strange about it and he'd barely taken a sip from his tin mug of tea as he stared into the darkness hour after hour.

Dawn would be soon.

He hoped that when the sun rose all he saw was barren rocky shores, the beating sea, and a handful of seagulls – just like usual.

If the morning light showed that, well, he'd drink down his tea and change the watch a happy man.

He made the sign of the bird over his chest at the thought, and gently stroked his necklace sewn of gull feathers. Seagulls were alert. They shrieked at danger. He'd always thought they were a good house for him. Even now in the Claws, where he wore signs of the Winged Empire, he still felt like his spirit connected to theirs.

They were quiet now but when dawn came, they'd be shrieking

and diving over the sea.

A bee buzzed around his mug and he tried to swipe it away. What was a honeybee doing here, miles from any flowers? He shook his head. Sometimes nature made no sense.

He smiled as the first blush of light peeked over the horizon, straining his eyes as he tried to see what couldn't be seen yet. The minutes ticked by and he let out his breath, waiting, waiting.

The sea still seemed darker than usual as if even the morning light couldn't banish the shadows this day. But that was likely only an old man's imagination after a long night.

The light bloomed a little brighter, picking out white shapes floating on the surface of the sea.

What in the …

The tin mug hit the tower floor, splashing cold tea over his polished boots. He didn't care.

The surface of the water was speckled with dead gulls. At the base of the tower and filling every bit of land he could see, was something dark and tangled. It clawed toward him like a bed of writhing snakes, creeping right up the sides of his watchtower.

Something shrieked with the dawn, but it was not a gull.

CHAPTER ONE

I flinched as Zayana dabbed a cloth over my injuries. Her posture was haughty, but her actions told a different story as she tended me.

"I managed to stitch the shoulder while you were unconscious, but I felt bad doing it without your permission."

I managed a faint laugh. "Better to stitch without permission than to let me bleed to death."

"You wouldn't have bled to death, but it wouldn't have healed well either," she said, worry in her eyes. "I wish you could spare some of your bees for *this* wound. I don't like the way it is so red and angry."

We were huddled in the bow of the boat as she nursed me. It was an old fishing boat, in good enough repair that I guessed people from the village had been using it frequently on the river. Ivo said he found it on the bank, stuck against a fallen tree in the water. It probably drifted downstream from where the town of Vlaren used to be before the Forbidding claimed it.

"Do you think the bees are actually healing his wound, or just keeping it stopped up?" I asked, shooting a glance down toward the rear of the boat and then quickly looking away.

"I see a spirit honeycomb inside his wound. It's the strangest thing I've ever seen. But there's no infection as far as I can tell.

He's feverish – but that's to be expected."

Zayana looked flustered, her court dress was rumpled, and soot-stained and little streaks of soot marked her face. I knew that I must look worse. She'd had to tear my shirt and jacket at the collar to get to my wound.

"I'll stitch the jacket when you can take your clothing on and off without pain," she said guiltily. "I really am sorry about them. I'm not much of a seamstress."

Her little bird cooed sadly from where she had it tucked into the neck of her dress. Its spirit feathers were torn and ragged.

"Is Flame getting any better?" I whispered. He'd been damaged in their desperate fight with the Forbidding.

She looked down, her eyes glassy. "I hope so – Wing Ivo says these things happen sometimes. That I need to work hard on invoking good into him to heal him, but he feels so real and so vulnerable. I just … I just don't know."

"He's like you," I said, offering a smile. "He looks small but he's resilient. He will heal."

She smiled ruefully. "I need to go see to my other patient."

I nodded and she made her way carefully to the center of the boat where Le Majest, the crown prince of the Winged Empire, the terror of Far Stones and apparently, my owner, lay with a sword wound to the belly. A sword wound that I put there. A sword wound that my bees filled now, holding it together and holding *him* together. A sword wound with a spirit honeycomb being manifested inside him. What might that mean?

I swallowed. If I had what my heart wanted, I'd pull my bees away and let him die. I'd get revenge for the death of my father and the threat to my family. But that wouldn't stop the Winged

Empire. And it wouldn't bring back my father. It would just doom my family, Zayana's sister, and all of our lives in a single stupid choice.

I looked past the crown prince and met the light blue eyes of Osprey as he stared at me from the tiller. He clenched his jaw and looked away.

"If it had been anyone else," he muttered. "Anyone else."

Like he was the one who should be angry! He attacked me! He fought me! And he ultimately sliced my shoulder, which was the only reason that it hurt like a Forbidding-taken bear right now! I should be angry at *him*. And I was. Sort of.

I was also very confused. Because even when he'd been attacking me it had looked like he was trying to save me in some way. What did you make of someone who both wanted you dead and watched you with eyes of hope at the same time?

Beside him, Ivo leaned in, speaking in a low voice.

"We won't reach Karkatua for days. We should find a place to spend the night. A place not filled with the Forbidding."

"Mmm." Osprey's reply made me want to look at him to see what had him so distracted, but I kept my eyes to the river on either side of us, flashing in the noon sun. A small tree grew in the crevice of the tall rock banks surrounding the water. It had almost no soil or land, and yet it grew. Relentless. That was what I had to be.

Creeping to almost the edges of the river, tangles of the Forbidding reached out, the edges of them waving in the warm breeze. For some reason, the Forbidding always avoided the water. It could creep down to the very edge, but not touch it. You couldn't push it back with water like you could with fire – we'd tried that before – but water was a place where settlers were always safe.

Which made me wonder why the people of Vlaren hadn't taken to the river. What had happened to that town? My feet itched to go back and find out. We never left homes or farms or towns taken by the Forbidding alone. If we couldn't reclaim them then all the able-bodied people nearby would organize a posse, fight back the Forbidding, investigate, and set the place ablaze if it could not be resettled. We never found survivors or remains of people – only buildings and sometimes evidence of how it had happened. Sometimes there would be food still fresh on the table, or a sword sticking out from a tree showing that settlers had battled the Forbidding here. Or sometimes there would be a tangle of Forbidding thrust through the floor of a boat where it was beached on the land, showing how the escape route had been cut off. Vlaren would have those signs if we went back to look. But we couldn't afford to do that right now and I doubted my companions would want to try.

"We need a place on a high spot, close to the water," Ivo was saying. "A place where the Forbidding is already back a bit from the shore."

"One with lots of fallen wood or driftwood," I chimed in. "So you can build a ring of fires around the site."

Ivo nodded, smiling slightly at me. "Any other tips?"

Osprey only pulled another pick out of his sleeve and jammed it between his teeth as if I didn't exist. One of his hands clutched his belly as it had been clutching it since I regained consciousness. He was hunched over it protectively. Maybe this whole situation made him feel as sick as it made me feel.

"We'll want to make a hammock for Le Majest if we can. He

shouldn't be on the ground."

That got Osprey's attention. His angry gaze swiveled to me and stayed there as something close to fury simmered in his eyes. *Snap*. The severed end of his toothpick tumbled to the floor of the boat.

"I'd say that anywhere away from you is the best place for him," Ivo said. "It will at least keep our Osprey from shaking apart at the rivets, hmm?"

I snorted. "Because you still don't believe me that he manifested snakes. That he tried to kill us with them."

"I believe he tried to kill you," he said.

"Just like *I* believe that trying to stop him has doomed us all." Osprey leaned over the tiller like a large cat standing over its kill.

"I wasn't going to die like that. And I wasn't going to let him kill you," I said defiantly. "All this honor of yours about avenging him is ridiculous."

"You don't listen," he said spitting the pick and leaning forward. "You're irresponsible and headstrong. I tried to tell you that our lives are not all that hangs in the balance."

"Oh, you've told me. And told me and told me. If I kill him, then you'll kill my whole family. And you'll kill me. You act like you're some kind of mindless tangle of the Forbidding who has no choice but to attack and kill. But you could just as easily say no and turn your back on your orders and spare my life. Killing me will be *your* choice."

He shook with emotion. "I keep telling you that I'm bound and you don't believe me. I was forced to drive you back, to nearly kill you – and if Le Majest dies I will be *bound* to slit your throat right here and yet, you foolish, frustratingly violent girl, you keep insisting on making the wrong choices and forcing us deeper and deeper into this mess!"

"They're not the wrong choices!" I said, hands on my hips. "Zayana told me how Wings given bird names are bound. She told me how your family will die if you don't obey him." Osprey paled but I pressed on. "And that's awful and horrible, but don't you realize that *you're* the one threatening my family with the same thing? However you feel about the Winged Empire, that's how I'm starting to feel about you. You keep saying that you don't want me dead but your actions back there spoke louder than any words." I paused. "I thought we were friends."

He started to stand and Ivo's hand whipped up, grabbing his arm and pulling him down. Osprey turned, beginning to snarl, but Ivo's tense posture stopped him. Ivo pointed with his other hand and all of our eyes drifted to the center of the boat where Zayana was carefully backing up from her patient.

A specter, glowing a faint emerald green – rose from Le Majest's mouth, rising up, up, up as its hood flared out. A snake.

"See?" I said, raising an eyebrow as I looked at Ivo and crossing my arms painfully over my chest. "Snakes."

It crept forward and as the last remains of its tail left the mouth of the crown prince, his big blue eyes flickered open. Everyone who wanted me dead had blue eyes.

He groaned and the snake snapped out at my bees. I felt a jolt of pain as it caught one, gulping it down.

I hissed and my bees shot up into the air, buzzing frantically.

"Control your snake!" I said, desperately, fighting against the pain in my chest and the buzzing so loud that it clogged everything else in my mind.

He let out a cry and wrapped himself protectively around his belly wound.

"Easy!" Wing Ivo cried. "Easy now!"

"Aella, bring your bees back." Zayana sounded frantic as she took a step toward the crown prince. His snake struck out at her and she barely dodged the attack.

"Control your manifestation!" I said again, nausea swirling through me as my bees spiraled over top of the boat, avoiding the snake but agitated by the attack and the loss of one of the swarm.

Juste moaned, his snake swaying wildly, and then collapsed, his body going limp and the snake fading out of existence.

I breathed a sigh of relief.

"Plug his wound," I told my bees.

They coalesced and filled his wound again as Zayana rushed over to help him.

"And that," Ivo said calmly, "is why this situation is so complicated, and why our next move must be the right one regardless of who is holding a grudge against whom."

CHAPTER TWO

We found a clearing in a patch of tall broadleaf trees. The trees surrounding it were so thick that we couldn't see the Forbidding, but that didn't make me feel any better.

"Where is my sword?" I asked as the bow bumped the rocks and hurried to scramble out of the bow and hold us steady. My shoulder screamed at the movement, but I gritted my teeth against the pain and fought the waves of nausea crashing over me.

"I have it," Osprey said, tapping his belt where he'd put my scabbard alongside his own. "And I'll be keeping it. You are too violent and liable to get us all killed."

He winced as he stepped out of the boat, still hunched slightly. Had I wounded him?

"I need it to fight the Forbidding," I said in what I hoped he would consider a polite tone. It was hard to be polite when I was so frustrated. My bees began to hum louder in tune with my flaring emotions.

Osprey opened his mouth, but Ivo laid a warning hand on his arm again. Did they do that a lot? It must be handy to have a backup conscience around to remind you not to be an idiot.

"How would you feel if I took it, Aella?" Ivo said gently. "I can battle back the Forbidding tonight while your shoulder heals up and then when you're ready for the sword again you'll know where to find it. As your Guide, I am bound to stick with you until your training is complete. You can trust that I am not going anywhere."

I noted that he didn't say he'd give it back. But at least Osprey wouldn't have the sword. I nodded sharply and grabbed the rope tied to the ring in the nose of the boat, wrapping it deftly around a tree on the riverbank and securing it with practiced knots. You did a lot of knot-tying on a homestead like mine. It felt natural and almost comforting to tie a clove hitch in the rope.

As I worked, I fought a sudden sharp memory of my father moments before his death – his single eye looking at me with the intensity of the sun on a summer day. I gritted my jaw against the pain of the memory. The rest of my family was out there in the Forbidding somewhere. Whatever Raquella had meant when she said that they had fled *into* the Forbidding – whether they were carving their way into it or had found some other way around it – couldn't be a good thing. It was too dangerous and there were too many of them for it to be more than a temporary solution.

I needed to focus on getting Le Majest to a healer and then I needed to convince Wing Ivo to help me go after them. He seemed like a reasonable person. More than anyone else here, he seemed to be on my side.

I fought back the swell of emotion and turned, only to step backward in surprise.

Osprey loomed over me, his bird manifestation fluttering at his back. It blocked the others from view.

"Zayana and Ivo are settling Le Majest," he said quietly, tucking a new pick into the corner of his mouth. One of his hands still cradled his belly.

"And you thought that meant this was a good time to come finish the job you started?" I asked grimly.

He sucked in an angry breath but then he closed his eyes, the muscle in his jaw jumping as he clearly tried to rein in his own temper. I felt a little thrill of satisfaction. I could stir him up as much as he stirred me up. That made me irrationally happy.

"I thought it was a good time to try to explain some things."

"Like how you want me dead?"

The toothpick went wild again. I tried to push past him and his hand shot out and grabbed my upper arm. I flinched as pain shot out from my wounded shoulder.

He gasped and let me go. "My apologies."

"For grabbing my wounded arm just now or for giving me the wound in the first place?" I crossed my arms over my chest. Jagged slashes of emotion ripped through me, leaving me gasping in their wake. Pain and betrayal were uppermost, but anxiety and attraction were mixed in there with them. I was too much of a mess inside to know how to feel about this man.

"I beg your forgiveness for both," his voice was low. He seemed younger with the formal words and the hiss of pain that followed them. "I do not want you dead, Aella of House Apidae. I *am* bound to kill you. But that doesn't mean I want you dead." I met his icy blue eyes and held his gaze as he spoke, the white pick dancing along his lips. He looked like a human osprey – a predator of the skies and sea. "I asked you to be my ally and bound you to me with an oath because I want Far Stones to be freed. I want this land brought out from under the power of the Winged Empire. But more than that – your bees give us hope that someone – anyone – might stand up to the dominance of a world of birds and live."

"That's a nice sentiment, but meanwhile you're trying to kill the person you claim inspires all this hope." I fiddled with my clothing, distracted. I only realized what I was doing when his eyes drifted down to watch my fingers picking at his osprey cuff. It had slipped out from under my sleeve.

He reached out slowly and touched the cuff, his finger trailing up and down the leather. He wasn't touching me, and yet it felt almost like a caress.

"I don't want you dead." He punctuated the sentence by looking up through his lashes at me in a way that made my heart stutter. What right did he have to look so pretty and young and at the same time be so infuriating?

"And yet you're bound to kill me." I let my cynicism leak into my tone.

"Only if he dies." He was clutching his belly again, a flash of pain rippling over his face like water. A wounded predator. I could practically see the feathers at the back of his neck ruffling.

"Are you … did I hurt you?" I asked, taking a half of a step forward. We were so close now that I could see the tension around his eyes.

He shook his head, but more like he was shaking off the question than like he was denying the hurt.

"Let me see," I demanded, stepping forward and grabbing the edge of his tunic. He sucked in a quick breath, catching my hand to stop me, but he didn't put much force into holding me still. I met his gaze and slowly lifted the edge of his tunic to look at his belly. The skin was unbroken and smooth. There was no bruising across the hard muscles under his clothing.

I frowned. He was acting like he'd been wounded, and yet there was nothing there.

"Maybe your ribs are broken," I suggested, but he hadn't been cradling his ribs, only his belly.

"It doesn't matter."

I reached out carefully and touched his hard belly, trying to feel if there was something I was missing that was hurting him. His dark skin was silky, but I felt nothing out of place. I frowned and withdrew my touch. He snatched my hand in his before I could fully remove it. A little shiver ran through me. Sometimes his sudden movements reminded me of how fast he could strike in attack. Like when he attacked me.

"I need to explain something." His eyes glowed bright, seeming to open larger as he confessed. "I didn't ask to be granted a name. I didn't ask to be made a Guardian of Le Majest. It was forced on me in a way so horrific that I do not speak of it. I am not my own man. Can you understand that?"

I nodded but I bit my lip. "My father said that once your fight is gone, there's nothing left of you. Have you given up on hope?"

One side of his mouth turned up in a sad half-smile. It brought a dimple out in his dark cheek. "My fight is not gone. I wouldn't hurt so much if it was. But I'm not free either. I'll be fighting for my freedom and yours for as long as there is breath in my body – but I also have to fight against other threats. I just … I want you to know that I don't want you to die."

"But you're also bound to kill me," I prodded.

"It's like there are two of me – the one that wants to keep you safe and watch you fly free and the one that is bound with heavy chains and being dragged along to watch your execution."

A look of desperation flickered over his features. He clenched his jaw and it stilled.

"To carry out my execution," I corrected.

He shrugged awkwardly, looking away for a moment.

"Which one will win?" I pressed.

His eyes seemed to burn, his fingers still resting gently on the cuff as if it was grounding him to me.

"I don't have promises that I can give you," he said. "But I do have something else."

He pulled my arm gently forward so he could access the cuff he'd given me, and with clever fingers, he opened a fold around the edge that I hadn't realized was there and parted the leather.

I gasped as it revealed a glowing purplish-white feather stitched to the inside.

"It's one of Os' feathers," he whispered, as if this was too important to say aloud. "When Os is close – which will mean that I am close – it will glow brighter. When we are far away, it will fade. A tiny piece of me will go with you wherever you are. It's the only gift I have to give right now."

It was a sweet gesture. And yet it hurt so much.

I pressed a hand to his chest and he gasped. I'd accidentally placed my palm right over the glowing feather embedded under his skin – the one I wasn't supposed to know about.

"I think that you and I will need to remain apart, Osprey. I can't see another way. You're bound to try to kill me and I'm determined to live. Which means that the most distance we can put between us, the better."

He looked away stiffly and nodded.

I folded the edge of the cuff over again and pushed past him into the clearing. I needed to think about anything other than that look in his pained eyes.

CHAPTER THREE

I didn't look at the others as I stalked to the edge of the forest and began to gather wood to light a fire. It would be night soon and we'd need a lot of dry wood to keep six fires going all night long. I threw myself into the task refusing to think of who my bees were protecting, refusing to think about who might decide to kill me out of duty, refusing to think about how much my heart hurt.

My head buzzed with a thousand thoughts and instead of embracing any of them, I let my mind drift in the buzz, just one bee among many.

I gathered wood intently, scraping every dry stick off the ground until it was clear of deadfall. Under one fallen tree I even found another snake carving. It looked like the ring around an old well. I dropped the log I'd been holding like it was a serpent and backed slowly away. I'd never uncover another snake carving without remembering that horrific scene in the cathedral under the ground.

I was finishing the last fire when Ivo approached me in the careful way you approached people who you thought might lash out in anger.

"Wing Ivo," I said respectfully, offering the sign of the bird.

He laughed a bit harshly. "That bad is it? You give me my formal name *and* the sign of the bird?"

I swallowed nervously.

"You'll make peace with who Osprey is eventually. We need him. He's an essential part of our cause."

"The cause of freedom?" I asked.

He looked over his shoulder carefully. He and Osprey both were being very careful not to discuss this near the prince or Zayana.

"The cause of the Single Wing."

I licked my lips. "My father told me to trust the single wing. I didn't know what he meant."

"I saw his tattoo as I readied his body. One of his boots slipped off."

I thought back, wondering if I'd ever seen my father's bare feet. I couldn't recall seeing them. I had no way of confirming or denying what he said.

"He had our mark," Ivo said. "He's as much a part of this as I am – as you are now."

"A part of what?"

"The revolution. The people who want to fly free of the Empire. These days, there are not many left and most of them are on the continent of Far Stones, which is why Osprey and I are intent on finally lighting the fires here and beginning the fight. He tells me that you're with us. That you swore in blood."

"I don't even really know what I swore to," I admitted. "I'm starting to think that I should know."

He nodded sharply and looked around carefully as if to be sure there was no one else around.

"The first settlers of Far Reach were mostly men and women who wanted their freedom. They wanted it badly enough that they hacked back the Forbidding and carved a life here for themselves – not completely free of the Winged Empire, that wasn't allowed, but far from the bureaucrats and laws of the Empire, far from the constant proclamations and injustices. They thought the distance would be enough, that the Empire would start to forget about them. And they did for a while.

"They raised families – like yours – and built a life here. I was with those original settlers. As a Wing, I have duties that take me back to the Empire for years at a time, but always I ache to return to this land. It's in my blood now, as I'm sure it was born in yours.

"But I digress. A few years ago, when the Emperor began to put added tariffs on steel and other products coming from the Empire to the colonies, we began to realize that the Empire had remembered us again. And that is never a good thing. They brought more Claws to Far Stones and set up a garrison close to Karkatua – where we are heading right now. And as the soldiers poured into our colony, the spirit of revolution poured through the people. We have clusters of the Single Wing now in every city and in every town, in most homesteads. If someone hasn't joined us yet, the chances are that they either haven't been reached by us or work directly for the Empire. Your father was among the revolutionaries. Likely, your neighbors are, too."

"But he never mentioned it until he was dying."

"Our strength is in our secrecy. We don't tell children under eighteen. Don't look at me like that. Despite all you've done, you're still a child and you're under my care."

"Then why are you telling me now?" I asked.

"I think the bees change everything. We need you for the revolution. The people need a spark point to push them to open action and the fulfillment of the prophecy will do that. All across this land, the news is being spread, people are readying themselves. We just need a few important elements before we can rise. So … don't give up on me, now, girl. You've made progress with those bees, certainly. And that is good. But we need you to go beyond what is reasonable – for the sake of the coming revolution."

I yawned – suddenly feeling exhausted.

"Yes," he agreed. "They sap your energy. But your life depends on keeping them working in the crown prince."

"Osprey will kill me if they fail," I agreed.

"More than that," Ivo said. "We will have need of them and you before you can possibly be ready. So, you must stretch yourself – and stretch the bees."

"I think I need to get away from Osprey," I said quietly. "I need to flee while I still can."

"Hmm." Ivo looked into the distance, brow furrowed.

"Would you … would you go with me?" I asked.

"It would be better if Le Majest didn't die at all. Or at least, not by your hand. Osprey really will be bound to kill you and he is a fearsome enemy. A real hunt by night, slash and dash, glory of the Empire kind of killer."

That wasn't making me feel any better.

"Which is why I think I should get a head start," I said.

"If you stay, the crown prince might live. We just have to get him to Karkatua. By boat traveling downriver, it will only take a few days."

I sighed. "But will you leave with me when the time is right? You said that as my Guide we had to stick together."

He chewed on his lip and then looked me squarely in the eyes. "By Wind and Flight, I swear it. I will stay with you and guide you. We will flee at the appropriate time and save our strength for the fight to come."

My mouth twitched into a slight smile and his answering smile was warm.

"Give it until Karkatua," he said. "It will be easier to get horses there and resupply anyway. If we have to leave in a hurry, we don't want to go on foot."

"And you'll stand with me over Osprey if it comes to a fight?" I asked, my arms crossing over my chest nervously.

"I will," he said gravely.

I nodded my head in relief.

"And now, let's see to the strengthening of these bees. You will need them."

"How?"

"Prayer or meditation. Find a way to reach out to what is beyond and join the song of the ages – or I guess the buzz of the ages in your case. That's the fastest way to improve. And we need you to go further than any new Hatchling can be reasonably expected to go."

I yawned again.

"Which is why," he said, "as much as I would like to let you rest, you must take first watch. Yell if you see anything, but spend this time meditating or praying. Reach into the skies above with your heart and let them reach back."

He was gone before I could tell him how crazy he sounded. Maybe this was why he'd never been a guide before. I made the rounds, checking the fires, toeing them in or adding fuel, and refusing to look into the center of the camp where the others spoke quietly over the hammock they'd made for Le Majest. How was I supposed to pray or focus on lifting my heart to the heavens when all I felt was utter rage and hot frustration?

I thought they were all asleep when I took up my place beside one of the fires, but in the darkness, I heard the faintest of whispers.

"If it had been anyone but her, I would have welcomed his death, avenged it, and we'd already be galloping toward revolution now. She complicates everything." That was Osprey.

"Women usually do." That was Ivo. "Would we even need to revolt if he was dead? Couldn't you –"

"No. The Winged Crown would still crush us even if the crown prince was dead. It would bind me tighter than I am bound now. Don't you think I would have found a way to see it done by now if that could save us?"

"You're no murderer, Osprey."

"Sometimes I'm not sure about that anymore."

CHAPTER FOUR

In the morning, Juste Montpetit – Le Majest – woke up with a vengeance. I was deep in sleep, curled on my side to prevent any weight on my wounded shoulder, when his threats woke me from a dream of my father.

"What madness is this? Tell me who has allowed it!" His tone was almost a shriek.

I sat up painfully, pushing past the loud buzzing in my head to try to hear his words.

"Get them off me! Off!"

He slapped at my bees in his belly, crushing one of them.

"They're holding you together," I gasped.

"Someone explain to me," the crown prince said in a low snarl, a tremulous finger pointing at me, "why she is still alive."

He twisted, shuddering with the pain of the movement, and then lunged toward me on all fours, like a wounded wolf. I scrambled backward over the trampled plants on the floor of the clearing, but he was shockingly fast. His hand shot out and gripped my throat. My bees buzzed around us in a cloud, as frantic as I was.

I gasped, clawing at his hand. My bees faltered, retreating to his belly. I didn't dare ask them to come to me. I knew what would happen if I did – death for Le Majest swift execution at the hand of Osprey for me.

"Le Majest," Osprey said with a deep bow and the sign of the bird – one clawed finger to each shoulder and then one to his head. "Her bees keep you alive. We cannot kill her without killing you."

Juste Montpetit fell away and I scrambled backward, clutching my bruised throat. He slumped, cradling his belly in his hands and watching it with utter horror.

"We must find another way," he said with a small tremor to his words. "I want to be rid of these abominations."

Was he afraid of my bees? The thought made me oddly triumphant. He only survived due to my mercy. I could remove it and render him useless. And then I met his gaze and all thought of triumph fled as I saw the cold calculation in them. If Osprey hadn't warned me before, it was easy to see it now – Le Majest would kill me as soon as he could do it without killing himself.

His eyes drifted down to where my hand clutched my throat and narrowed as they settled on the exposed cuff there.

One of his eyes flickered, almost like a flinch, and then a ghostly snake uncoiled out of his eye – there but not there – drifting down to his shoulder.

His eyes fluttered and his head arched back as a low moan escaped from his lips. I swallowed, ready to remove my bees if that snake looked like it might lunge toward us. But the power was too much for him. He fell bonelessly to the ground.

Zayana rushed forward, checking his eyes and listening to his heart. "He needs a real healer. And he needs one quickly. I'm not an expert, but I've been with ailing relatives before. I would guess we have days – at the most – before he dies. These bees holding him together are not enough. "

Osprey and Ivo exchanged a look that seemed to be full of a question I didn't understand. Neither of them had moved. Their birds hovered above them like banners.

"Tend to the prince, Hatchlings," Ivo said. "I need a word with Osprey."

I clenched my jaw. Whatever they were going to say, I wanted to hear.

Zayana's eyes widened as she looked at me as if she was trying to tell me something with just a look.

"What?" I hissed as the two Wings walked down to the water's edge and crouched together on the riverbank, their birds shielding them from view.

"You have an opportunity here," she whispered as she put a balled-up cloak under Juste Montpetit's head and began to lay him out gently. "This morning, I awoke to a blue cloud passing over a white one. A sign of change and portents."

Her hands avoided the swarm of bees over his belly, holding his guts together with their spirit honeycomb. I shivered, looking at them. Imagine what it would feel like to have moving, creeping bees inside my belly. Even though they were mine, the thought of that gave me the creeps.

She glanced over to the murmur of Osprey and Ivo's voices before laying a hand on Le Majest's head for a moment. "You could win his favor. His life depends on you right now. Which means you can't change your bees to a bird the way he hoped.

But maybe you can make him your friend. Nurse him to health. Make yourself invaluable. When he recovers he'll remember and reward you."

"Like he rewarded your family for their loyalty?" I hissed. "Your father was slain!"

"Not by the crown prince." She frowned. "Listen, I know he killed your father. I know that is hard to bear. But he has good intentions for the Winged Empire. He wants to make it a place of peace."

"Then why all the bloodshed?"

Her frown deepened. "He confiscated all the weaponry from the people to keep us safe. Once he gets back to the continent, he'll send for more Claws and they will make the people here safe, too."

I shuddered. The idea of more Claws flooding across the Far Stones made me ill.

"He manifested a snake and tried to kill me."

"He wasn't in his right mind. He'd just seen horrors no man should see."

I shook my head. Did she really believe that? Or was she just convincing herself of it because following a maniac was too much to stomach?

"I think he should be honored that you are caring for him," I whispered. "But I do not think that he will feel that way about me. I'm going to tend the fires."

She looked worried, but I avoided her gaze as I toed in the nearest fire, pushing the fuel into the center as we let it burn down. No need for another forest fire. I tried to look casual as I made my way slowly toward where the Wings were whispering together. Whatever they were talking about involved me. I shouldn't be kept out of their conversation.

"…want to leave now. While I still can," Ivo was saying. "You know as well as I do that the Quills will be growing anxious. We need to get word to them."

"You can do that when we reach the coast and find a healer," Osprey said in response. "Until the prince is …" His words were whipped away in the wind. I strained to hear more. "…so she must stay with him until then."

"The moment those bees are out of his belly, you'll be forced to fall upon her and destroy her, friend. I want to spare you both – and spare the Far Stones. We need her bees."

"I'll find some way," Osprey said grimly. "Give me time to think of what that way might be."

"You have until we reach the coast," Wing Ivo agreed. "But after that, I must flee with her if you haven't found a way – and risk the chance that you might follow."

They made the sign of the bird grimly and I focused twice as hard on the fire I was toeing in, trying to look absorbed in the task.

Osprey met my eyes as they broke their huddle and he frowned, his toothpick moving from one side of his mouth to the other with almost frantic intensity as his gaze burned into me. He had his belt knife out and he was carefully cutting white toothpicks from a length of sapling. The way he went through those, he must have to do that a lot.

I tore my gaze away from him and back to my work. Ivo wanted to split off from him – a solid idea. And Osprey wanted to find a way not to kill me but still stay with us – a risky plan at best. But what did I want to do? I needed my own plan to get out of this tangled mess.

"Working on your meditation, Hatchling?" Ivo asked as he gathered up his few things. The sun was over the trees and it was time to get back on the boat.

"Yes," I said, but the thing I was meditating on was how Osprey could feel like my ally and my enemy all at once and if there was any way to get away from the crown prince now that my bees were tangled up with his life.

"Good thinking. We need to be moving. No sense wasting any more daylight."

We loaded the boat with the unconscious crown prince and what little we had. Between Osprey and Ivo's packs, there had been two bedrolls. Both were being used now for the comfort of Juste Montpetit. There were also two waterskins, a few small items like woods knives, flint, rope, string, some bandage rolls, a little hardtack, some dried meats. In Osprey's bag – to my surprise – there had been a tiny pot of honey and a lace-edged handkerchief. He'd blushed when Zayana found those, and I wondered if there was a lovely lady back on the continent worrying over her handkerchief and the person to whom she had given it.

The sun was bright as we launched the boat onto the deceptively calm water of the river.

I perched in the bow, keeping an eye out for rocks just under the surface or rapids ahead.

"We've been lucky so far," Ivo said. "But rapids are bound to be somewhere on this river. Every river has them."

He had the tiller, Zayana had the care of the crown prince and Osprey was talking to his bird.

"I'll scout ahead when I can," he said quietly before he put his forehead to the bird's and began to whisper to it, his hand gently caressing the bird's feathers. I couldn't help the stab of jealousy that shot through me as he rested his cheek against the bird, running a hand gently over its feathers.

I should know better than to let myself watch that. Osprey was a threat to me not a … what? A friend? That felt too weak to describe the tang of emptions I tasted when I watched him with his bird. It also didn't explain why I kept glancing over my shoulder at him even while I returned to my job, trying to hide my furtive glances. I couldn't deny my attraction to him – as much as it made my cheeks grow hot. I tried to tell myself that there was a good reason I was curious. After all, since I first met Osprey he had flown everywhere on the back of that bird – almost obnoxiously so. It was strange to me that he wasn't flying ahead or getting help, just whispering to this bird. It was almost as if he was staying here on purpose to be near us. That was a good reason to be curious, right?

The boat jostled as the hull lurched across a rock.

"Are you blind, girl?" Ivo asked me from the back of the boat. "Or are you meditating so deeply that you can't do your job?"

"Apologies!" I called back, focusing again on watching for rocks, but I couldn't help obsessing over what had changed that bound Osprey to the boat. Was it the hurt crown prince? Or had he lost so much energy that now his bird could not bear him?

I focused on the water, my gaze drifting from time to time to the riverbanks. Many snake carvings decorated the edges of the river. At one point I thought I saw an old, crumbled footing of what had once been a bridge made of thick stone snakes. At another, someone had carefully etched them into an overhanging rock. I tried to ignore the creeping sensation that rolled over me. There was nothing I could do about ancient relics.

As we traveled downriver, the Forbidding grew thicker and more intense, twisting the trees and rocks along the edges of the river, sometimes right down to the water. Was I imagining things, or was it moving? Writhing and wriggling like snakes?

I shivered.

But the feeling did not leave, and after an hour I began to worry.

"Have you spent a lot of time in Far Stones, Wing Ivo?" I called back.

"I have a home in Astar Harbor," he called back, but he sounded distracted, too.

"Have you ever seen the Forbidding look so … alive?" I asked, trying to keep my voice calm.

Ahead, the river narrowed, suddenly. Rock walls rose on either side of the river. There was no way to go but through the narrow channel between them where the water sped up, tumbling over itself as it rushed between the rocks. I looked around, desperate for somewhere to beach the boat, but everything was thick with the Forbidding, tiny strands of it waved out over the river as if searching for prey.

"Hold on to your heads!" Ivo cried from the back. "It's going to be rough!"

We plunged into the rushing water at the same time that a bright purplish-white bird burst out over my head, rushing before our boat.

"Os will see if there's a waterfall ahead," Osprey called over the roar of the water reverberating off the stone walls.

A solid plan. He might be able to stop our boat with help from Ivo's golden eagle. Or maybe they could help bear it down the falls gently so that no one was hurt or killed. I clenched my jaw and braced myself against the boat, wishing for the first time that my bees were fully under my control so I could send them to look for me.

The net dropped out of nowhere.

CHAPTER FIVE

It filled the gap in the rocks in front of us, unfurling so quickly that I only had time to give a wordless cry of warning.

Ivo swore and his eagle sailed into the air like an arrow loosed from a bow.

There was an odd, wailing sound.

I looked over my shoulder to see figures dropping down from the side of the rock, holding ropes.

No – not ropes. Glowing, spirit snakes.

Zayana screamed as one of them snatched her up, his snake twisting around her body and binding her arms to her sides.

Five more attackers were in our boat already as I struggled to my feet, feeling for the short sword that wasn't there. I pulled my belt knife instead, lunging toward the nearest figure. This was why you didn't take a girl's sword no matter how "violent" you thought she was.

The man nearest me had stone-grey skin and he was dressed entirely in snakeskins and emerald-colored scale armor. His green eyes glittered in the light as he lunged toward me, his snake darting beside him as if it might sink its teeth into me.

I slashed at the snake and it dodged back. I lunged after it, but the snake's manifestor grabbed my arm, pulling it behind my back and wrenching it up so high that I yelled in agony. I tried to kick back, but he increased the pressure, pinning me in place.

My eyes flicked over to the others. Osprey's bird dove down between the rocks, snatching up one of our attackers in his talons and flinging him against the rocks. He hit hard, falling lifelessly to the water with a splash.

Osprey pulled his short swords, leaping up with a growl in his throat. He leapt at the same moment that his osprey dipped under him. Os spun slightly as Osprey landed on his back, eyes up. A look of shock flooded his face a half-second before a silver net landed over him and the bird, dragging them back to the floor of the boat.

Another craft rushed down the river behind us, sealing the route out of the narrow chute in the river. Men and women dressed in scale armor stood in the bow of the boat, their expressions grim and their long polearms pointed toward us.

Ivo's bird reared up, its powerful wings knocking three of the warriors from the prow of the boat.

"Surrender!" the man holding my arm yelled out across the boat. "Surrender and you may yet live."

A pair of snakes rushed down from above, snatching up Juste Montpetit from the bottom of the boat. They curled around him, rising slowly into the air with his unconscious body cradled in their embrace. His eyes flickered open slightly and his own snake emerged – this time, coiling out from his ear. It curled around the other snakes almost affectionately and their glow brightened with the touch.

My stomach flipped at the sight.

"No moving!" my captor barked, jamming my arm harder behind my back.

I grunted in pain, sweat breaking out across my brow. My vision went black for a heartbeat and then returned in time for me to see Osprey shoving his swords back into their sheathes with a sour grimace on his face. He met my gaze and winked – one of those harsh winks that I was starting to think were his way of saying "hang in there" more than anything playful or secretive. He jammed a new toothpick in his mouth. Would he ever run out of those things? Os rose from his shoulders and passed through the net. He rose, up, up, up past the rock faces and the snakes and high into the sky as if to escape all of the chaos.

Behind Osprey in the rear of the boat, Ivo's hands were raised, a dozen polearm blades tickling the edge of his neck.

A long snake manifestation slithered down, dangling in front of him, its tongue darting in and out of a too-large mouth. I swallowed and then it struck, wrapping itself fiercely around his waist and shooting upward into the tangled trees above the river.

"Please," I said, worried now. "Please don't say we all have to go up that way. We don't mean any harm."

I was starting to hate snakes almost more than the Forbidding.

A snake dropped down beside us and my captor moved so quickly that I gasped. He released my arm, wrapping his arm around my waist and grabbing the snake in the other hand. My feet were ripped from the ground as we rose into the air so fast that my breath caught in my lungs. The boat was below me, the net holding in place as white water frothed around it. A glowing yellow spirit-snake dipped downward toward Osprey.

I opened my mouth to scream but the harsh voice behind me said, "No screaming or I'll hit you over the head."

And then we were stumbling onto the ground above in a single slash of open space between waves of Forbidding. The land twisted on either side of us, splitting into ribbons and curling or spiraling in every direction as if infuriated by our presence. The man holding my waist released it, moving his grip to my upper arm so he could direct me forward. He stepped toward the Forbidding and I froze.

His harsh laugh sounded sincere as he dragged me toward the tangle, his spirit-snake sliding before us like a rolled out rug. The moment his snake met the Forbidding, it stilled, seeming to part for him.

I tried to look back, to see what they'd done with Ivo and Osprey or where they had taken Juste and Zayana, but my captor pulled me roughly forward.

"Where are we going?" I asked him.

Was he taking me away from the group? What was he planning to do?

I tried to feel my bees, but everything was a blur mixing with the buzzing in my chest.

"You have one of ours in that boat. And we keep what is ours," my captor said roughly.

"And the rest of us?"

"He'll tell us what to do with you."

I almost snorted at the irony. Even when Juste wasn't conscious, what he wanted ruled. Even when crazy grey-skinned people emerged from the wilderness dressed in the skins of snakes – it was still what he wanted. There was just no winning with him.

CHAPTER SIX

I hardly had time to gasp and a blindfold was jammed over my eyes. I shivered. It was probably more snakeskin.

My hands were lashed together, and I was pulled by the arm through the woods – with what I could only imagine was the Forbidding or more of those horrific snakes tangling around my legs. My stomach lurched at the thought. Something snagged my foot and a spike of fear shot hot through me. What were they going to do to us? And who in the world were these people? My captor spoke with a strange accent and his clothing was unlike any I'd seen before. Wouldn't we have heard if the Far Stones had been invaded?

"Aella?!" the call sounded far away.

"Zayana!" I called back. "Are you hurt?"

"I'm fine," her words were a little breathless. "Do they have Le Majest?"

"Yes," I called back. Her loyalty was unshaken – as always. I would have thought that his snake manifestations would change that.

My captor tugged me roughly. "No talking. I would not like to stretch your pretty neck, but I will if I must, bird girl."

I opened my mouth and pain blossomed across my cheek. He'd hit me. I clenched my jaw tightly and tried to focus on what I could feel, blinking past the pain. We'd all been captured. That meant no one was coming to save us. I'd have to think of a way to get away from these people – whoever they were – on my own.

I felt for my bees. They hummed in Juste Montpetit's chest. He was ahead somewhere. I could feel that. I could hear grunts and a cry of pain that sounded like Ivo. I twisted my hands against my bonds. Pain blossomed as I was cuffed across the cheek again.

I sucked in a long breath. Maybe I'd wait before testing my bonds again.

It felt like we'd been traveling for a long time when the air around us grew cooler. It felt damp against my skin. I tried to think about what that could mean. Were we near a hidden pool?

Something sounded louder ahead – something that sounded like the murmur of voices in a language I didn't understand. My captor said something in a harsh language with short, sharp syllables.

And then I felt something on my ear. A bug? No – too large. I tried to reach for it, but my hands were tied. Tried to rub it away with my shoulder, but a hand hit my shoulder hard enough to bruise and then the thing – whatever it was – was sliding into my ear. I screamed and heard other screams echoing my own. The same sensation bloomed in my other ear and then it was gone, and I was left trembling.

"Screaming over the gift of our snakes? How did you think that would win our pleasure?" my captor asked, his harsh voice seemed to suit his words now. "I refuse to continue to speak your filthy language and translation will only make this more difficult.

Better to give you new ears immediately."

He ripped off my blindfold and I saw him swaying slightly as if exhausted. A long rope of snake slid back into his hand.

"Why did you blindfold me?" I asked boldly. He kept pulling me after him despite his loss of energy.

"I hate it when captives squirm," he said. "It makes the whole thing take forever. And there are places that you should not see."

"Did your snake … did it go inside my ear?"

His answering laugh held a nasty note that set my teeth on edge. The constant buzz in my chest rose, growing more and more irritated. So, he liked letting his gross snakes slither through people, did he? Well, maybe I'd show him what bees could do.

My captor took a sudden turn and threw me to the ground as if he'd sensed the violence welling up in me.

I hit hard on my wounded shoulder and moaned, struggling to get up again with my hands still tied behind my back. I pushed up to a sitting position and found Zayana sitting beside me, her eyes wide with terror.

"Are you hurt, Aella?" she asked.

"Only a little," I said through gritted teeth. My shoulder screamed with pain. I'd probably pulled the stitches. But there were no new injuries. I blinked back tears at the sharp pains radiating from my shoulder and tried to look around us. "Do you see any of the others?"

Our captors had disappeared back into the tangled landscape. Were they planning to leave us here? But then why do the snake thing to my head?

"Just Le Majest. They had him on a litter made of spirit snakes."

"Ugh. Did they put a snake through your ears?" I whispered.

Zayana shivered but she nodded, her Imperial face carefully cold and distant. "Who are these people? I wasn't told about invaders here."

"I wonder if they *are* invaders," I said, working at the bindings behind my back. They felt like a rough jute twine. If only I could get at my belt knife. "They seem to know their way around."

There was a crash in the distance and a long scream. Something slashed through the trees above us. Another scream. Then stillness.

Zayana shuffled toward me and I leaned into her, trying to look in every direction at once. "Is Flame hurt?"

"No. I have him hidden. And your bees?"

"I can't tell," I admitted. "I'm not very good with them yet. I could call them …"

"…but that would leave Le Majest in danger," Zayana finished. She nodded as if agreeing with me that he should not be disturbed. "I knew there would be trouble. I should have said something. There were four turtles on a rock in the river. Four! An even number. Nothing could be more inauspicious."

Something rustled through the tangled Forbidding ahead of us. I focused on the sound, trying to keep my breathing even. Trying to keep from panicking. We shouldn't be able to sit so safely in the middle of a tangle of Forbidding. I should have realized it would come for me soon.

I swallowed down fear. I was House Shrike. I was relentless. I would not let fear take hold of me.

There was a crashing in the dark Forbidding ahead of us and then a swarm of men and women in masks dragged an unconscious Ivo to where we were, tossing him on the ground like a sack of bones. I gasped as one of them kneeled on his back, lashing hands and feet together with brutal efficiency. There was no sign of his eagle.

"What are you going to do with him?" I asked, my voice trembling more than I would like.

The snake-masked attacker closest to me backhanded me, splitting my lip. I spat blood, blinking as pain shot through my head.

"Silence."

If they thought beating me would make me docile, they were wrong. The pain was awful. But I was House Shrike and we didn't cower or bend.

They left again, and this time, when they returned, they had Osprey, still tangled in the net, but unconscious, head lolling to the side, his familiar toothpick nowhere to be seen. The net had been strung to a pole and four heavily muscled men lifted the pole to their shoulders.

I swallowed, thinking of a bird I'd seen one, caught in a net. The poor thing hadn't stood a chance.

They marched into the Forbidding, Osprey's limp form swinging between them, as a second group grabbed Ivo and threw him into a similar net. I flinched as his limp body fell heavily onto the ground as they moved him. That was going to leave bruises. In moments, his net was attached to another pole and four more bearers carried him into the Forbidding, their masked expressions blank and unyielding.

A pair of them grabbed my upper arms, wrenching me to my feet at the same time that they pulled Zayana up.

"Where is Le Majest?" she asked, her voice shaking. I expected them to hit her, but surprisingly they did not.

"You ask after the Adder? Your concern is admirable. His snake has given him a fever and so has that poorly patched wound. We take him to the temple of the Cobra for healing and harmony."

I stared at the one speaking to her, wishing I could see behind the mask. Temple of the Cobra? Adder?

A grim realization was starting to flood over me. We were the Winged Empire – as much as I both feared and hated that – and we were people of the skies and of the birds. My belt had shrike feathers sewn to it. My knife had a shrike etched on the handle. Birds or feathers, wings or claws decorated every bit of clothing we wore or owned.

These people – in contrast – were masked as snakes, wore the skin of snakes, and manifested snakes that snatched us from our boat. Was it possible that the underground cathedral we'd been in – the one that Juste Montpetit Hatched in – was one of their temples? Was it possible that they had been here in the Far Stones all this time, leaving deep in the earth or far into the Forbidding where we did not know to look? Perhaps, they the ones who built the bridges covered in snakes, the ones who decorated old monuments with them. Maybe they were even the ones who made the Forbidding in the first place.

I shuddered at the thought, but my suspicions only solidified as we were marched through the gnarled forest. Those who led us thought nothing of walking between waving tangles of Forbidding. They walked up the sides of waves of land that curled over and around. They ducked and hunched as they walked under spirals of grass growing overhead instead of under their feet. But the twisted land didn't harm them. It even seemed to move away from them, curling away rather than toward them as they moved.

I watched with rapt attention. What made it respond to them differently, and could I find a way to make it respond to me like that?

Imagine how far you could go in the Far Stones – how much you could do! – if you didn't have to constantly battle the land!

We hiked for hours through the tangled mess. The path – if there even was a path – wove in and out and up and down through such thick, swirling landscape that I was lost within the first hour. Even the sun didn't seem to behave as I expected. It should be midmorning by now, and yet it hadn't moved at all.

I was starting to grow more concerned, when my captors stilled for a moment, looking up and I followed their gazes to something rising out of the tangle of Forbidding before us.

Four stone snakes rose, tangling together in a spiral tower as they reached an apex where their carved heads split out in four open-mouthed images, each looking in a different direction.

We began to move again, and the twisted ground parted, revealing steps upward to what must be the Cobra Temple. Snakes formed the steps in coils. They lay one on top of the other so that the stairs wound around the building, sometimes forming strange S curves rather than a straight flight of steps.

All these snakes left a creepy feeling under my skin. Snakes would think differently than birds. Where a bird would choose a direct path, a snake would choose a twisted oblique approach.

It was long moments before I realized that some of the carved snakes decorating the steps leading up to the open-sided temple were not snakes at all, but more masked people wearing light scale armor and belts of snakeskin banded across their chests.

I tried not to stare as we were led up the steps, but the sense of being squeezed was becoming more and more powerful as I ascended. It was all I could do not to panic.

Just like with the underground cathedral, the snakes across the steps were carved in such sharp relief that they seemed to almost be alive. Shadows rippled deep and dark between the carved snakes so that it seemed as if we were walking up steps of snakes instead of stones.

Zayana stumbled beside me and we shared a brief worried glance. Whatever came next couldn't be good. Ice flowed down my spine, settling into my belly.

When I fought the Forbidding all those years, had there been people like this hiding within it? Did they watch as I lit fires in their tangled mess? The Forbidding was more my enemy than anything else – more than Juste Montpetit and the Winged Empire even. It had been fighting me since before my first steps. I'd always thought it was a mindless entity, like thorns or wildfires. What if it wasn't? What if it had something to do with these people?

When we reached the last few steep steps and could see the top of the platform, I froze. Osprey and Ivo – still unconscious – had been lashed to two of the snake-pillars, encased from neck to feet in wrapping spirit snakes which were longer and thicker than any snake I'd ever imagined. They glowed a light green and the one resting his head almost lovingly on Osprey's chest seemed to wink at me.

Not good. Of all of us, Osprey and Ivo were the most

powerful. And there was no way they could escape from that kind of confinement even if they were conscious.

Which meant I needed a plan. A plan to use my bees to get us all out of here.

And I needed it quickly. They set Zayana up against a pillar and the warrior closest to her went slack suddenly, his eyes rolling back in his head and then a spirit snake rolled out of his mouth and down to the ground where it began to wind around Zayana's feet, moving slowly upward as it bound her to the pole.

Did all of them have snakes? That would make each of them equivalent to our Wings. I'd have to fight or evade all of them to escape.

Sweat slicked Zayana's forehead. She stared straight ahead, trying not to flinch but she couldn't stop a small moan of terror from rippling from her lips.

"If you think I'm going to let you do that to me, you can think again," I said, scrambling backward. I hit a hard wall and spun. One of the guards was right behind me.

I could call my bees – and risk losing Juste Montpetit's life – and then Osprey would kill me when he came to – if he came to. Or I could try to run and risk being beaten into unconsciousness. Or I could submit and hope that if I did that, they would spare me.

Too many ifs.

"Come," I called to my bees and the buzz in my chest rose powerfully. I felt them gathering and moving. It left a sensation of satisfaction rippling along my skin. I held my breath, anticipating their return to me.

There was a cry from the other side of the temple and a

woman in a high-collared scale armor suit leapt up to the temple level waving her hands.

"Which one pulled the bees away? The Adder is bleeding out!"

"I did," I said calmly, as my bees buzzed toward me, encircling me in a friendly cloud.

"Send them back," she ordered.

"I won't be tied up," I said grimly.

She looked down the steps on her side and then back at us.

"Untie her. She won't go anywhere. Release the bees to heal the Adder, girl, or you will be slaughtered over a long seven days. We shall start by showing you how we can twist your very flesh from your bones like the twisting of the land."

I clenched my jaw and whispered, "Return to him. Heal his wound."

Loss flooded over me as my bees obeyed, streaking out from me and back toward my enemy. No bees, then. But at least I wasn't tied up. Perhaps I could steal a weapon.

Hands clamped down on my arms.

"Don't even think about defying them, property," a cultured voice drifted to me.

Shocked, I looked to see Juste Montpetit stepping up over the edge of the steps to the temple platform. Sweat slicked his forehead and fresh blood stained his coat around his middle, though my bees buzzed in his belly. He walked slightly hunched, both hands clamped around his middle. His eyes glittered with hate when they met mine.

CHAPTER SEVEN

"The Adder," reverent gasps echoed around me as the rest of the snake-masked people climbed the steps and circled the platform. They formed rings around the platform on the top two steps and on the very edge of the platform, leaving the center of it open.

A long moment passed as if they were waiting for something. Juste Montpetit looked around at them, swallowing as he held his belly together with both hands. His snake materialized, poking its head out from his eye and slithering down to ring his shoulders like a scarf that had slipped.

There was a hiss, and then the crowd parted slightly and a figure in high-collared gold scale armor stepped through. He towered above the rest and his snake mask had a hood around it – like the hood of a cobra. Snakeskin belts crossed and re-crossed his chest and hips. His polearm ended in a long, serrated blade that curved in a way that made me think of snakes. Its handle, similarly, was a long ripple like a snake in motion.

He ripped his mask off.

It must have been a signal. The moment the mask was gone those around me ripped their own masks off, dropping so suddenly to one knee that their armored knees made a clatter against the stone steps and platform.

A chill shot through me. These people were so organized. They'd materialized out of nowhere. They wore snakes as their sign. This could not be good.

The snake man nearest me tried to pull me down with him, but I kept my feet, fighting his grip. I would not bow to them. Just like I would not bow to Juste Montpetit.

"Brothers," the tall figure said, and a ripple of pride bloomed on the faces of those around him. They were shockingly pale – almost grey-tinged. "We stand today in the sun for the first time in fifty years." Well, that explained the pallor. They should get out more. No, scratch that. They should stay underground. "We stand according to the words of prophecy and visions of our seers."

"We stand!" The crowd boomed. Which was ironic since they were kneeling.

"In the words of the great prophet, Ica'ar, *The Great Day Descends. Long did we wait for the son of Wings and War to come to us. From his mouth pours wisdom and his eyes behold greatness. He shall come from afar and light the path for the ascendancy of the snake, the great day of the Adder. He shall rip down their wings and snatch them from the sky. He shall shatter the sun and bring back the darkness. All will bow before him in his shadowed glory.*

"And Ha'vat likewise spoke in prophecy, *Out of the adder, something to eat, out of the snake, something sweet.*

"Today, in our midst, we see the Adder rise – a child of the Winged ones by body, but a child of ours in spirit, he comes to us!"

"He comes to us!" the voices around me thundered.

I tried to be subtle as I turned to look over my shoulder. The steps were full of those kneeling and more bodies climbed from the Forbidding to join them, seeming to emerge out of nowhere. There were probably two hundred people here with the crowd growing by the minute. An army of people.

I couldn't fight so many people. Tension rippled through me like a blade. I needed a different plan.

"Our seers," the tall man cried out, "Foresaw this would come today. At this time. In this place. On this river."

I frowned. Really? Or did they simply have very good spies? Anyone could have told them where Le Majest was and what he was doing. But these people could not blend in enough to spy and even Juste Montpetite could not have known he would manifest snakes a few days ago. I risked a glance at him and saw him staring at me balefully, triumph and vengeance warring in his eyes as he battled the pain in his belly. One of his arms was braced against a pillar, stiff as a tree, propping him up straight. It left a smear of blood where it had slipped slightly.

I swallowed, my mouth suddenly dry. This would only make him more powerful – more able to crush me. And I'd given him even more reason to want to with that slip.

The man in gold clapped his hand on Juste Montpetit's shoulder, his grip tight on the other man. And fast as lightning, a snake poured from his ear and darted into Juste's ear, linking them somehow. The man in gold's eyes widened and a look of bliss settled over his face. I shivered as his expression was mirrored in the crown prince. They were sharing something beyond words – something brought on by the snake. Revulsion rolled through me like a mudslide.

"I, Ixtap, leader of this Tentacle, speak true," the tall man said. "We have found the Adder. We will bind him to us today in sight and clarity."

"Bind him!" the crowd called.

There was a sound like stone grinding and the center of the platform began to move, sinking very slowly, inch by inch.

The snake linking the two leaders remained in place, glowing a sickly greenish-yellow. Juste stumbled slightly, his hand on the pillar slipping more.

"Do you have a healer? I am mortally wounded."

The woman who had yelled at me before emerged, running her hands over his body. She offered him a drink from a flask and looked to Ixtap as he drank, shaking her head.

"I cannot tend him here."

"The binding is too urgent to wait," Ixtap said. Beside him, the platform continued to sink.

"What is the nature of this binding?" Juste Montpetit asked, his chin tilted up arrogantly. There was a glassy look in his eyes as he swayed slightly. "Does my manifestation not mark me as your chosen one?"

My eyes widened. He was going to get himself killed.

Ixtap's face became stony. "It marks you as the Adder, most certainly. The prophets are not wrong. But our tradition tells us, '*All who bring forth the snake must be brought to the heart and must suffer.*' You have brought forth the snake. You will now suffer."

"I am honored to be among you." Juste Montpetit's words were honey even as he swayed, pale and feverish, against the pillar. "It is as if I am seeing clearly for the first time. I envision a great rule over all the earth – benevolent and generous. No one will be in need for the Emperor will guard and guide them into truth. I envision no more need for war, for all those with violent hearts will be censured and taught humility. I see peace and prosperity for a thousand years." He paused, scanning the crowd. "After a brief burst of violence, of course. The snake must first strike if his juices are to fill the prey."

"Strike!" the crowd cheered from their knees, raising their fists. Of course, they liked that part.

The center of the platform had lowered a hand span now. I watched them, nervous by the gleam in their eyes. They had not liked the talk of peace and prosperity. Perhaps they would have liked it more if they knew what that meant for Juste Montpetit – peace for those who bowed to him and conformed to his every whim. Prosperity for himself in his palace. But they did not know that, and they only seemed excited by the prospect of striking. A dangerous people. And they had me in their grip.

Where had they come from? This temple appeared ancient.

Juste Montpetit tilted his head to the side, his eyes narrowing in thought. His hand slid a little more down the pillar, his knees wobbling.

"Your prophecy also stated that wisdom would pour forth from my mouth. Hear, now, my wisdom." He paused dramatically, his face filling with a beatific smile that suited his wide eyes and flushed cheeks so well. "I am greatly weakened, struck down by the sword, these pitiful bees the only things holding me together. Unless you have a great healer here, the healing properties of the bees must be maintained." He looked around but when no healer was offered, he continued. "And yet, the keeping of your tradition is valuable to me. I respect all traditions. I honor them in my soul." It was all I could do not to roll my eyes at that. "Therefore, it is my wise judgment that a way must be found that will preserve the health of your Adder but also honor your traditions. I choose the way of the substitute. I offer you my property – Aella of House Shrike – to take this suffering in my stead. She will bear it for me, even as her bees bear the weight of my life."

Wait.

What?

There was silence as the crowd waited for something. Ixtap's expression turned to a frown, but the snake glowed brighter as he looked Le Majest up and down. He must have seen as easily as I did that Juste was barely holding himself conscious.

"This breaks with tradition, Adder. What is seen in the heart is a sacred thing for the minds of the Hissan only. How can we give such a thing to a stranger?"

"She is no stranger to me, Ixtap. I can see you are a man of honor. That when you call, warriors assemble. That when you say 'go' they go and when you say 'stay' they stay. And so I call on you to see that this girl is my substitute in these things, hands for me, feet for me, eyes for me. She will go as I say 'go' and stay as I say 'stay' and what revelations she is given will be for my heart only."

There was a murmur in the crown and nervous shuffling. Ixtap frowned, his eyes turning inward. A woman broke from the crowd, her golden chains jingling as she rushed to Ixtap's side and whispered in his ear. It was the healer from before. After a moment, he nodded. He made a swirling sign like the letter "S" in front of him.

"We will accept this claim of substitution as our traditions confess, 'he who takes on another's suffering is that man for that time,' so we allow the substitution of this girl for the Adder."

There were more murmurs and no one sounded happy – though they weren't nearly as unhappy as I was.

Ixtap raised his arms again. "By your honor, I call you to this. She will serve in his stead."

The crowd responded with a grim roar. "IN HIS STEAD!"

My stomach dropped. No, no, no. I did not like this at all.

"It will not kill you," a voice said beside me so quietly that I almost missed it. I glanced down to see one of the snake warriors who had brought me here looking up at me. His snakeskin vest and snake-leather belts marked him out. "Probably. But it will hurt a lot. The mind rejects what is done with it and it fills the body with pain in defense."

Oh, great. So they were going to do something to me that was so awful my own mind would rather be in agony than in whatever they were going to do.

The snake binding the two leaders vanished.

"Most people survive it," the helpful voice offered.

"What a heartfelt assurance. That's so good to know," I replied, dryly. I fought the violent urge to be sick. Only Juste Montpetit would cheerfully sign someone else up to suffer for him – and of course, it would be me.

He raised his arms with enormous effort – more sweat breaking out across his brow as he did – and smiled at the crowd, turning so he could see them on every side and then strode toward me, carefully skirting the center of the platform which had lowered as deep as my knee.

When he reached me, he leaned in close and his grin turned sadistic.

"What a tidy solution to two problems, don't you think?" He whispered to me. "You shall secure me a powerful ally and it won't cost me a thing. But know this, property. If a single bee leaves me while you suffer, I will kill your friends here – the little Hatchling with the bird, the fool Ivo, maybe even my own guardian. So – no flinching. No losing focus. Keep your healing bees on me or they'll pay the price."

I felt as if all the blood had rushed from my head. I swayed slightly.

"I see you understand," he said, his eyes narrowing with malice. "I shall enjoy what happens next."

His hand shot out so fast that I didn't even flinch before it was wrapped around my throat. With a powerful wrench, he threw me into the center of the platform. I stumbled over the lip, falling into the center of the platform and skinning my knee and palms on the snake carvings. I clambered to my feet just in time to see Osprey stir, his eyes opening and a look of horror filling his face.

CHAPTER EIGHT

"Osprey," I whispered as the platform began to descend even faster. It was waist deep, then shoulder deep, descending so quickly that I couldn't find my bearings.

He straightened in the grip of the spirit snake holding him and his mouth opened at the same moment that my stomach dropped and the platform fell from underneath me. I clawed at the air, a scream ripping through my throat, and then something slammed into me, wrapping around me, and bearing me upward.

I looked down, hoping beyond hope that Osprey had sent his bird to help me.

Horror filled me instead, as I realized a giant sprit-snake – larger than the carved ones holding up the pavilion roof – had me in its grip. It rose from the dark depths. I stared down its coils, realizing that I could not see where the snake ended. It could be miles long. It could eat me in a single gulp. Sweat slicked my forehead and back at the thought. I leaned over, heaving up everything I'd eaten over the last day. It didn't matter. The snake's coils rose upward, bringing me with it.

I wiped my mouth with the back of my hand and looked up. Its head – powerful and massive – was just above the spot where it gripped me in its coils. I felt darkness press on me, threatening me with unconsciousness, but I didn't dare let it. If a single bee winked out with me, my friends would die.

I tried to reach for my belt knife, but my arms were pinned to my sides by the snake's coils.

Don't panic, Aella. Don't panic.

Anxiety welled up in me, threatening to overwhelm thought.

Hold on. Aella. There will be a way. Don't lose your head.

The invocations I was saying to myself weren't working. My breathing sped.

The snake rose slowly, as if stretching out the drama of the moment. As my head cleared the pit again, I met Osprey's gaze. Relief flooded his icy blue eyes as they locked on mine.

"Be strong," he mouthed and winked, which was not at all reassuring given what had happened the other times he winked at me. But I met his gaze and refused to look away, hoping that somehow, just by watching him, he could give me strength.

Something purplish-white flickered beside his head and then was gone again. Os. His bird. Was something wrong with it? A look of pain flashed across his face but before he could respond, I was dragged further up by the snake and I lost sight of him.

The crowd clung to the steps of the temple on every side and spread like spilled molasses into the Forbidding tangle beyond. What had been two hundred before was at least a thousand now. My breath caught in my throat at the sight of all these people in gold scale and snakeskin, masks pushed up onto their heads and pale eyes staring up at me.

My dry throat ached. My fingers itched for action. The buzz in my chest grew so powerful that I could hardly hear anything else.

"Today, we witness your clarity and pain on behalf of the Adder. You shall be his eyes and his conscience from this moment forth!" Ixtap cried.

The snake squeezed around my middle and my eyes bulged as all the breath was squeezed from my lungs. Panic rose in me as I reached for my bees, reached for the buzz that was fading by the second.

Relentless, Aella. Be relentless.

Darkness shuttered over my vision and with it a burst of agonizing pain.

Then light.

A great tower soars up through the trees. It is spindle-thin, but it widens at the top to form a shelf where a man sits in a cage made of white snakes. Ravens fly to him with food in their mouths. Satisfaction fills me. With their general caged, they must leave our shores. All the death has not been in vain. I have not spent my magic too freely. I am growing old. Another will need to pick up my mantle.

Darkness flooded over me, erasing the vision and I was back in the grip of the snake. Stabs of pain rippled up through my arms from my fingertips. I bucked against the bonds of the snake, a scream tearing from my lips.

Something hisses in my ear. I look out over a seaport with dozens of white sails in the distance. Behind me the Forbidding crawls, whispering to me with the hiss of the ages.

"The land rises against them. They cannot stay forever," Malit, my right hand says from beside me. His eyes are red-rimmed, aching from all this exposure to the sun. "Come, General Tavit. Let us retreat into the earth. It is almost time for the seasonal slug-run and my mouth waters. Besides, your first child is expected. There will be

time for conquest when he is born."

Darkness again. This time it came from my eyes and pounded through my head. I wrenched one of my arms free, tearing at my own eyes. Please, make it stop! Please!

I am watching people pouring off a boat. Two of them hold birds aloft as if they are falconers, but these birds glow in a way only snakes should. Revulsion rolls through me and I begin to hiss.

"We must tell the elders, Tavit." The voice is behind me. Sesra. I know her voice like my own. She has enchanted me utterly and one day I shall convince her to bear my children. Malit says I'm a fool for hoping, but he is wrong.

"We'll tell them tonight when they give me my belt," I say quietly. They will be pleased with the results of our first scouting mission. We've found something so odd that honor will be ours.

Darkness. Pain. Pain so deep there was nothing else. Nothing but the spark of a melody sizzling into he pain, soaring like the flight of an eagle, dipping like the plunge of an osprey to the sea.

I am deep below the earth. A sense of wellness fills me. I hold my child, Tavit, in my arms. He is so tiny, born only yesterday. Around me, my snake Grenor slithers happily, tangling through the room and around my chair. Tomorrow we begin the At'ap'pur. Tomorrow we cleanse this land of all manifestations except the Great Snake we worship. And after that, who knows?

"The world awaits our dominance, Fa'al," my wise woman says.

"So let it be."

Darkness. My bones felt as if they were breaking within me. My throat was raw with screaming. But still, the song was there, carrying me upward toward the skies with loving waves rippling over each other. It reached a crescendo at the same moment that

I felt I would break apart. I closed my eyes, abandoned the pain and sank into it. Another voice joined the song, soaring upward, upward, upward.

Light.

We look upon the earth. It crawls now in a terrible tangle of what once was, perverting it, ruining what was once beautiful and right.

"It rejects us," Va'at says bitterly. "Our own land rejects us."

"There are ways to make it bend to our will, to make it part for us," I say, determination thick in my voice. I'm not so eager to retreat beneath the ground as my brothers are. "We have discovered them. We will discover more given time."

"Why fight a battle we've already lost?" Va'at's bitterness is contagious. "Our own land has rejected us. We are nothing now. Nothing but those who creep beneath the earth."

"It labors like a woman with child and one day, it will produce something new," I say. But I'm not sure. I'm not sure of anything anymore except my need for revenge.

Darkness and pain. I sought the melody and found it immediately, clinging to it, clutching it in both hands and with all my soul. It carried me, tucking me under its wing. I leaned into it.

The tree in front of us was moving. Little shivers played up and down my spine. This couldn't be.

"The Land itself is manifesting," Ha'vat, our wise woman is saying. Her snakes ripple up and down her arms, their tongues flicking.

"Manifesting what?" I ask as my son Fa'al plays around my feet. He tugs at my boot, his baby face smiling up at me.

"Not snakes," she says. "Something else. Something I've never seen before."

"Will it harm us?" I ask, looking down at my little son.

"Who can say?" she shakes her head. "But I have a prophecy. A time is coming soon that will leave all parents sad they bore children. All the old look back on hard times thinking they were soft. It comes on eagle's wings. But do not fear, for I have another word with it: Out of the adder, something to eat, out of the snake, something sweet."

"How delightful," I say.

Darkness. But this time, the pain has lessened and there is only the song.

CHAPTER NINE

I gasped in a long breath, clutching my throat with my free hand. My throat was ragged and agonized as if I had been screaming for hours. My vision returned slowly from the darkness. First, just as shapes and then slowly colors that wobbled and ran together like berry juices mixing.

The snake began to lower me, and a spike of panic rolled through me. I did not want to go back to the center of the earth. I did not want to be swallowed up in a world of snakes. But I had no strength to fight. My whole body was wrapped by coils of snake except one arm and it felt like jelly, wobbling and formless.

I clung, still, to the melody as the colors began to solidify and clarify. The snake people were still kneeling around the temple, but the sun was sinking low on the horizon, only a faint orange glow was left. The melody soared as I was lowered to platform level. I could finally make out who was singing. My eyes met Osprey's as the melody tumbled from his soft lips, soaring again as his gaze met mine with determination and strength behind it.

Had he sung all this time? Had he sung me through the pain?

I kept my eyes on his, lapping up the strength in them, pulling it into myself as the coils of the snake released me to the platform floor. I tried to push myself up, but my strength was gone. Everything was thick and heavy. I couldn't grasp my own thoughts. My emotions ran through my fingers like water.

The song faded on a last, lingering note and a sense of deep loss filled me as it fled.

Osprey bit his lip, his eyes still locked on mine.

Ixtap cleared his throat and lifted his arm above me. "The suffering has been met. The clarity has been given."

Juste Montpetit stepped forward, so close to my prone body that all I saw was belt and chin. He lifted his fist in the air. Ixtap's face went stony and he paused for a heartbeat before taking the crown prince's fist in his. It mattered to him that Juste Montpetit had not taken the test himself – that much was clear. But for some reason, he had allowed it.

I swallowed against the pain in my throat, trying to gather my strength as the pain slowly faded away. It was over. I was free of it. I sucked in long, cool breaths, grateful it was over.

"You will eat with us tonight," Ixtap declared, clapping Le Majest on the shoulder. Juste swayed at the contact, my bees buzzing furiously within his belly. "Swear your followers to non-violence, and I will release them to wait for you with your watercraft in the new place where we have put it."

"We are dedicated to non-violence," Juste Montpetit said grandly. "My followers will obey all your traditions."

He promised away our lives so easily.

"We celebrate!" Ixtap announced.

"Celebrate!" the crowd echoed and as one they rose to their feet again, pushing their masks down over their faces.

I groaned. I didn't feel fit to stand, never mind make that long trip back to the beaches.

"I'll give them a guide," Ixtap was saying to Le Majest. "But they must swear not to manifest their birds on the journey. And they will be blindfolded on the way to the river. They will be free to take you where you wish to go once you return to them, but we do not trust them as we trust you, Adder."

"Agreed," Juste Montpetit said softly.

"Le Majest," Osprey gasped, the snake binding him tightening at his words. Pain etched his face as he objected. "My duty demands –"

"Nothing." Juste Montpetit cut him off. "Your duty demands nothing but that you obey. The great Warriors of the Snake are not my enemies. You know the cost of defiance."

There was a rattle as those warriors hit their polearms to the ground in emphasis of his words.

"Be grateful that they spare your worthless lives on my behalf." The corners of Juste's mouth curved slightly on his pretty face as he said that, and I wondered if it was to woo these new friends of his. Their ululating responses suggested that they were flattered. "Wait for me at the riverbank until I come for you."

He snapped his fingers and then they were on us, wrapping blindfolds around our eyes as the rest of the crowd cheered Juste Montpetit.

"Are you always so excited when a snake manifests?" I asked the warrior blindfolding me. My voice was weak, but my curiosity was not.

"When it's one prophesied generations ago? Yes."

So, we both had prophecies about us and people depending

on us. I had more in common with Le Majest than I would have thought.

The warrior tried to drag me up to my feet, but I could not force my muscles to stand. Even trying to sit was too much. I collapsed on the ground.

"Skies Fury!" he cursed.

"Let me," that was Osprey's voice. I felt gentle hands on my face. "Aella?"

"It's me." He must be blindfolded, too.

"Are you hurt?" we both asked at once.

"I'm fine," his hands gently found my shoulder and followed it down my side to my hip. The soft touches were oddly comforting. "But you can't stand."

"I'm trying," I said, exhausted just from speaking.

"Let me," he repeated, hoisting me up in his arms, I couldn't even reach out to touch him but he cradled me to his chest, one arm under me and one arm hugging my head and shoulders to him.

"You can't. Not for long." I tried to object.

"I will help," Ivo said, his voice sounding weaker than I thought it would be.

The crowd was moving away so rapidly that it was easier to hear everyone now. Zayana was sobbing softly in the background.

"Not after the beating you took," Osprey said firmly. "Hatchling Zayana, see if you can get an arm under him."

I heard a thunk and a curse and then Zayana. "I've got him."

Her voice sounded strained.

"We're ready to follow you, guide," Osprey said.

"I'll tie you to me," the guide said, no sympathy in his voice. "Keep up or I'll have to pull you along."

Time seemed to drag out as Osprey carried me down the steps and into the tangled Forbidding. I could feel his breath gusting from exertion, stirring the hair on top of my head, but he never once complained or slowed.

"Hold on," he murmured into my hair.

"Os?" I asked.

"Will recover," he replied. "As will Harpy. They were overwhelmed by so great a force."

The guide ahead of us made a satisfied sound in the back of his throat.

"My bees," I whispered grimly.

"Flickered in and out as you passed out in that snake's grasp," Osprey's voice was hard as flint.

"Will they hold when I am so far away from him?" I asked. If they didn't, the man who was holding me so tenderly now would slash me apart in a heartbeat.

"The farthest I can hold Osprey is a league. But I am very strong." His whisper was grim. Resigned.

"And you don't think I will hold them that far," I whispered.

But I would. I could feel it. Because hadn't my little bee flown all the way to my family and back? That was much more than a league.

"I hope for better things," he said, a small hitch in his voice betraying his doubt.

Behind us, I heard Zayana and Ivo murmuring to each other.

"What happened to Ivo?" I asked thickly. I was growing so weary I could barely keep my eyes open.

"He's a man of honor," Osprey said.

"How did that get him so hurt he can barely walk?"

"When he came to and saw you held by that snake, he fought so hard that they had to pummel him into unconsciousness again to make him stop," Osprey whispered. "I think he has broken ribs. But he will recover."

"Ivo," I mumbled, humbled by his sacrifice.

"He did the right thing," Osprey said there was a note of regret in his voice.

"So did you," I murmured. "Your song kept me alive. I thought only songbird manifestations gave you the power to sing."

His low chuckle rumbled through his chest. I closed my eyes and leaned into it.

"Sleep, House Apidae," he whispered. There was a note of gentle sadness to his words. "I shall bear you safely to the river's edge."

CHAPTER TEN

I woke to bright sunlight and the sound of water flowing. My mouth was dry as sawdust and I tried to swallow and my throat stuck unpleasantly.

"Aella!" Zayana's gasp of relief eased something in me that I didn't realize was tense with anxiety.

She was curled up on her side in front of me as if she'd been sleeping there. I pushed myself up enough to look around. We were laying on a thick layer of dried reeds along the riverbank and the rush of the river filled the air, lapping up against the boat tied there.

"Are you okay?" I asked her. Her bird was in her hands, looking a little stronger and a little less ragged than the last time I'd seen it. She was holding it close to her face. Had she been whispering to it before I awoke.

"I'm fine. Just anxious," she said, looking around. "Though I shouldn't be. There are three yellow reeds among the green ones on the riverbank. That's a good sign."

Beside us, stretched on the reeds, both Osprey and Ivo were laid out. Their birds weren't visible. No one had even lit a fire. It was as if they'd collapsed there as soon as they'd arrived.

"No sign of Le Majest yet," Zayana whispered. "I've been

checking on Ivo and on you through the night. Whatever they did to you seems to be mostly mental. I couldn't find any wounds to bind except for your shoulder. Ivo was brutally pummeled – mostly around the face and shoulders. I stitched what I could and bound what I could, but he needs a real healer."

I offered a half smile. "Thank you. I appreciate the care. Who would have thought a High'un like you would be so deft with a needle?"

Her answering smile was half-hearted. "I've been sitting here all night and thinking. All my life, I thought being a Wing was a unique thing. That the magic of the Winged Empire set us apart from other nations – made it reasonable that we dictate to them how to live. I thought that the strength and beauty of our bird manifestations was what proved that. But then your bees manifested. And then Le Majest's snakes. And now here we discover that there have been people here all along with snake manifestations. Maybe the birds aren't as unique as I thought. What does that say about the world?"

"That it's full of wonders?" I suggested.

She snorted. "They slaughtered my father to make my manifestation stronger, Aella. They took my sister as a hostage to use against me. And Flame is nothing. I mean, he's amazing, he's everything, but he isn't Os or Harpy. He isn't this powerful, impressive thing. He's just a little songbird. And the ruler I prostrated myself before – the one who will someday rule the Winged Empire – he manifested a snake." She shuddered. "What does that mean for the Winged Empire? What does it mean for Wings? Will he replace us with those snake warriors?"

"I don't know," I looked around the tiny clearing, wondering if anyone was listening to us. "I couldn't guess what Le Majest might do with more power. But I know what he did with a little power and it was chilling enough."

"I need to think," she said grimly. "My thoughts are a tangled mess and I need to think. I need to decide who I am."

I nodded and rose, managing to clean myself and brush off the worst of the dirt from my clothing and hair. I settled on a rock by the river when I was done, too tired to get up and walk to the others, letting my own thoughts drift out over the water. The things I'd seen – layers of one thing over another, spanning generations – had left their mark on me. So had the pain. And in the middle of the pain, the only true thing that had held me together was Osprey's song. What did I make of that?

I felt like I didn't fit in my own body right now. I felt like the world I'd known – with it's rules and ways – was utterly foreign, hurtling down a mountain like a tumbling stone and my only option was to hold on and try not to be crushed in the constant roll and shift.

"Still alive, House Apidae?" I was surprised to see Osprey joining me, stripping off his heavily embroidered jacket and plunging his head into the water. He shook it from hair and shoulders energetically before jamming a new pick between his teeth.

"Thanks to you," I said, pulling my hair back and beginning a careful braid to move it out of my face.

He pulled a knife from his belt, whistling as he started to carve a piece of stick into long white toothpicks. The song he whistled was the same song as the one he'd sung to me back at the temple.

"What's that song?" I asked.

"A song of subversion and rebellion," he said with a rueful

smile. "A song that reminds us we are alive."

"I'll remember it always," I said fondly.

He froze for a moment, a look of pain flashing over his eyes as he hunched over himself. After a moment, he shook himself and went back to whistling.

"Were you hurt?" I asked. "Like Ivo."

"No," he said, refusing to look at me. "My binding chafes. That is all."

"You look hurt. You're curled over your belly. You should let me look. Maybe you broke something. Maybe you're bleeding inside."

"I'm fine." His words were clipped.

"If it's my fault, then I want to fix it," I insisted. "Can you honestly tell me, it's not my fault?"

I tried to grab his tunic, but he pulled back, raising a warning hand.

"I said, 'no' and I meant 'no,' House Apidae. I am a man of honor and I bear my wounds with honor, too." He looked older than nineteen when he said that. Maybe the weight of his responsibility left him older inside.

"I don't understand what that means." I cleared my throat. "But I know that you're hurting, and I want to help. Maybe my bees –"

"Your bees are doing enough." One corner of his mouth quirked up with his words. "My mother was extremely fond of bees. She kept them in hives in her garden and gathered honey."

"She did? What was she like?"

"She was … not what anyone expected. Brave. Kind to me. Clever and scheming with everyone else. She married my father in a whirlwind romance and I was born very soon after. They say that she didn't so much as flinch when they slit her throat. That I should be proud that all her life force was channeled into making it possible that I might hatch."

"And are you proud?" I asked quietly. That certainly didn't describe how I felt about what happened to my father.

"Mostly, I'm just filled with despair. Until recently." He looked at me, and his blue eyes were bright in the morning sun. "Hope does strange things when you've lived so long without it. It makes you ache in places that just felt dead before. It makes your heart race with fear. It makes every second seem precious and fragile. I'm not sure I even know what to do with it now that it has dawned in my heart."

I almost felt like I could feel his hope echoing in his pain.

"Your song is what gave me hope in all that pain last night. It kept me from falling apart."

His smiles were so slight that sometimes they seemed like ghosts I was imagining. "I would have fought, too, if I thought it would do any good."

"And if you weren't ordered to stop."

His smile fell away. He swallowed, clutching at his belly again.

"I think you should let me look at that," I pressed.

"I think you've done enough," he said sharply, wincing in pain.

"What have I done?"

He shook his head, reaching into his sleeve to find another

toothpick, but he just held it between his fingers, turning it round and round.

"What have I done, Osprey?"

His eyes met mine, pain searing across them. "You want to know about how I am bound? What you do to him, you do to me. You stabbed him, and he's slowly dying of the wound. Even with your bees holding him together, the fever is taking him. I feel every burst of agony, every long gnawing pain. I feel it all."

My mouth dropped open. What strange magic was that?

"And if he dies?" I pressed. "Does the pain stop?"

His laugh was bitter. "This pain will stop, but by my bond I will be forced to avenge him. And do you think my pain will truly stop when I've placed you in the ground with everyone you love and with this brand new hope I thought I'd never have again?"

"I didn't know," I whispered. "There must be a way to break the bond."

He looked away from me, silent.

"I saw your feather," I blurted out. "We stopped for a rest just before we saw the town and you opened your tunic to look at your chest and it was there – glowing."

His mouth dropped open and the toothpick fell out. He didn't replace it.

"I saw it and I know that's some kind of magic. Does it have to do with the bond between you and Le Majest?"

"Aella, I –" He shook his head, stunned. "I …"

I waited for him to keep speaking, but he just shook his head.

"There's no feather," he said.

Which was a stupid thing to say to me because I didn't like liars. I crossed to him so fast that he didn't realize I was there until I'd jerked open his jacket and was pulling his tunic open.

"Wait –" he began, but I did not wait.

I opened his shirt.

The feather glowed bright under his skin as his eyes met mine, wide with guilt and fear.

"There is a feather," I said, tapping it with a finger as if to prove my point. His skin over it was blazing hot.

He clenched his jaw as if trying to keep the words in.

"You don't understand," he said.

"Then tell me."

He shook his head and though I waited, he only clenched his jaw so tightly that the muscle bunched and jumped.

"Tell me."

"You wouldn't understand," he snapped, breaking the pick in his fingers in half. "You wouldn't … you might not be able to focus properly on the revolution if you knew."

It sounded like a weak excuse – which it probably was, but there was more than anger in his eyes. There was bone-deep shame.

I sighed. "I want to see if I can help Ivo. Zayana says his face is badly hurt."

He jerked his tunic and jacket closed, covering the mark of his bond.

"I would have fought for you against the snakes if I thought I could have saved you. I swear it." He ran a hand over his short hair, looking away in an agitated fashion, but his other hand grabbed my wrist. He looked so vulnerable without his toothpick. "I … I care about our alliance."

I stepped back and he released my wrist. He cared about our *alliance*? My face flushed hotter. Here I'd been silly enough to think he might care about *me*.

"I tried to offer you the help that I could," he said desperately.

I narrowed my eyes. "Well, thanks for caring about our *alliance*."

I made sure not to look at him as I walked away, ignoring his call of, "Apidae!"

I found Ivo lying on the reeds and I sank down next to him. His face was a mass of bruises and cuts, his eyes both swollen to slits.

And they'd said his ribs were broken. Tears filled my eyes as I leaned over him, my hands hovering as I tried to think of what to do for him. He'd suffered all this for me. Just like my father had suffered and died for me. Just like I knew my family was suffering now, fighting their way through the Forbidding. Heat seared my palms and a golden glow ran from them as a few tiny bees fell from them.

I gasped.

"Please, help him," I begged them. "Mend his face, bind his ribs. Be strong but gentle. Be full of hope and mercy."

My invocation stirred them, and they fell to his prone form, buzzing as they reached his face and side. They began their work at once, congregating where the flesh was split and over the break in his ribs. I chewed my lip as I watched them. I knew without knowing how that these weren't the ones who had been healing Le Majest. I could still feel them far away like a faint echo in the mind. These were somehow new bees, as if my capacity for them was growing. I swayed from the weakness that poured over me as they stole my strength, channeling it into their healing efforts. They could have it all. Every bit of it.

I didn't know how long we sat there, but eventually my bees settled into the hard work of knitting him together, and I fell back on the reeds beside him, head swimming, gasping for breath. It had taken all my energy.

By the time evening fell, there was still no sign of Juste Montpetit.

We'd passed the day quietly, each absorbed in pain of their own. The experiences of the temple replayed themselves again and again in my mind. I relived watching settlers come to Far Stones, I remembered every detail of the moment the Forbidding first arrived. I thought hard about the generations of Snake manifestors and what it was they wanted from Juste Montpetit. But more than anything, my mind wandered to the Wing with the two ravens who was imprisoned in the tower. Who was he, and why did he look so familiar?

Ivo awoke while we were lighting the evening fire. Osprey had caught five fish in the river. He didn't tell us how and I hadn't seen him go off to fish, but we cleaned them in pained silence and wrapped them in leaves and mud to bake. We set Ivo up on a fallen log beside the fire. He gasped whenever he moved, but the bees had already made a difference for his face – I could only hope that they'd heal the ribs in time as well.

He waited until Zayana went to the river to draw water before he spoke. "And now we are in a jam, my fellow revolutionaries.

We planned to fight a battle on one front to be rid of our oppressors only to find that we might have one on two fronts."

"Is it still worth it to fight?" I asked. How could we defeat both enemies? We were unarmed, with none of their resources.

"You made a vow," Osprey said soberly. I almost rolled my eyes.

"I'm just asking," I protested. "Maybe there is a better place to find freedom than on a stretch of rock already claimed by two other powerful groups."

"How do you know that the snake warriors are powerful?" Osprey challenged.

"Are you saying they are weak?" I shot back. "After how they bound you without a thought and kept you from your bird."

His cheeks grew dark and I knew I'd struck a hit with that.

"Enough," Ivo warned, glancing over his shoulder. "This complicates things, but it doesn't change our hopes or goals. We will fight and we will carve out a place for ourselves and our brethren. But we don't have much time. We need to talk." He turned to Osprey first. "I think you'd be sad to kill our Aella now that we've gotten to know her."

Osprey grunted his agreement as if he didn't even want to bend enough to speak. I shot him a spiteful glance. He could at least pretend to care.

"And we both know she is the figurehead we've been waiting for," Ivo said.

"Even now that there are snakes manifested?" I challenged.

"Especially now," Ivo's face was grim. "Which means we need a plan. The crown prince will order her death the moment he doesn't need her anymore and you will be bound to carry it out, Osprey."

Osprey looked away, the bitter twist of his mouth only disguised by the toothpick he was fiddling with.

"We need to get them apart as quickly as possible. The moment we get to Karkatua, I want to split up."

"Why not now?" I asked. "Why not leave while he's with the snake people?"

"They watch us," Osprey said, eyeing the trees around the riverbank. "At least twenty of them. If you so much as move, they'll be on you."

Ivo nodded. "We'll wait for Karkatua. It's better if Le Majest finds a healer first, anyway. We don't want him to die. She can leave her bees with Le Majest for as far as they'll stretch and I will claim I need her on an errand out in the wild lands. You'll have to keep an eye on Le Majest, Osprey. Keep him busy while I steal her away."

"And if he won't be kept busy?" Osprey asked.

"Then we'll lose her, and with her, everything else."

CHAPTER ELEVEN

We spent a second night tending to our manifestations. Osprey walked down the riverbank first, his bird flaring to life in a burst of bright purplish-white. A moment later a song drifted upon the wind, rolling and bittersweet. And as he sang, the bird grew and preened. Os stretched his wings, running his beak down them as the song ruffled his feathers, bringing out their gleams and sparkles.

"That," Ivo said, "is one good way to restore your bird, Zayana. Have you been taught it yet?"

He sat gingerly, his side still paining him. I tended the fire as Zayana drew her tattered bird from the neckline of her dress. Ivo clicked his tongue sadly.

"Poor thing. It took a beating."

"How could it be harmed?" I asked him. "I thought it would just diminish if it was attacked. But it's actually hurt like a real bird."

"*He* not *it*," Ivo corrected. "*He* can be diminished if Zayana wears herself out, or if she forbids him or does not invoke him correctly. He can also be injured because our manifestations are more than pure magic. We put a little of ourselves in them. There is some of Zayana in this bird already, newly hatched though he is. And we will help her restore him tonight. I heard you singing harmony back in that snake temple, Zayana."

"You did?" she asked, her almond brown eyes going wide.

"You think I was so busy fighting that I didn't hear? You made a contribution. You joined Osprey's song of restoration."

"What's a song of restoration?" I asked.

Ivo pointed down the riverbank. "It's what he's doing right now. He's restoring Os. And when you, Zayana, joined him in restoring Aella," he pointed at each of us in turn, "you were using that same skill. Which should make it easy to use to restore your bird."

"I thought only words could invoke a manifestation," she said timidly.

"What is a song but words that dance?" He winked. "Try it."

She cleared her throat. Paused. Shook her head.

"We are making you nervous," he said with an encouraging smile. "Why don't you walk upriver a bit? Stay out of trouble but get a little distance and let yourself go. Be free. Sing to the bird and see what happens."

She nodded eagerly and stood, hurrying through the waving rushes.

"And now that leaves you, Aella," Ivo said.

"I'm no singer," I said warily.

He laughed and then moaned, his hand moving to clutch his ribs. His words choked out. "Then let's try something else. Something selfish."

"Selfish?" I pressed.

"For me, at least," his eyes glittered.

"Your bees have healing properties that I didn't guess were there. I should have. Bees have been healing people for centuries. And your manifestation of them is very strong. Do you know why that is?"

I shook my head. "I'm not much of a healer. My sister Raquella did that."

"It's because you know right from wrong. It's hard to correct what is wrong if you don't even know it when you see it. It's hard to heal anything if you can't tell what broke it."

"What should I do?" I asked, scooting nearer. "I don't even know how they started healing in the first place."

"Work on your invocations. Speak to your bees of things that heal – of warm summer days and blooming flowers, of the way we will rebuild the Far Stones when it is ours free and clear."

I looked around nervously. "Can we really make the Far Stones free, Ivo? It was hard enough to imagine when it was just the Winged Empire we would have to fight for this piece of rock. It seems even harder now that we know there is another enemy beneath the surface – an enemy that sees this land as theirs."

"Don't lose your fight girl. Osprey says you have family out in the Far Reaches."

I nodded.

"We're doing this for them and for all the people who long to be free. It's in us – this sky-given desire to chart our own courses to be our own people to make our own mistakes. It's in every pulsing, thundering beat of our hearts, in every gasp of our breath. It's the air we breathe and the song we sing and nothing's ever going to stop us. They can come at us. They can carve us up and spit us out and we'll still be singing our freedom song."

The melodies of Zayana upstream and Osprey downstream tangled in and out of his speech and for the first time in a while, I felt a thrill of hope.

"How do you and Osprey stay hidden?" I asked. "How do you work so closely to High'uns and Le Majest without being discovered?"

"A gift," he said, eyes twinkling. They were less swollen than yesterday. "The skies see all, and they have granted us a tiny piece of that seeing. We know who to trust. We know who is reliable. How do you think that Osprey knew to trust you? To bring you in on the most important, most life-threatening, most freedom-inducing project of our lifetimes?"

"I have no idea how," I said, somewhat bemused. I still didn't know what to make of Ivo and his grand speeches half the time.

"The Single Wing," Ivo said. He pushed his sleeve up and tapped his wrist where a single wing was tattooed there. "It acts as a guide. Gives you a little pressure to draw you in the right direction. We're all marked with it – all of us who long for freedom and the lifting of the yoke."

"Can I have one?" I asked, thinking of my father and how he told me to trust that mark. I missed him so much that it ripped through me at the strangest times with almost crippling echoes of emptiness. I felt a pang of it now as I asked for the sign.

Ivo chuckled. "You should have the mark! All free people should! But we'll have to wait until we can give it to you. Not here. Not now."

"Will you really get me away from Le Majest?" I asked, my voice sinking to a whisper.

"If any man can, I will."

"And then what will we do? We'll need an army to take Far Stones for our own."

He nodded. "An army of citizens ready to seize their freedom."

"But that won't be enough," I said decidedly.

He lifted an eyebrow. "Why not?"

"For the same reason that my bees are not enough to heal you just by buzzing around. They need direction. They need a leader. And we need a war leader. A general."

"Yes," Ivo said, gazing off into the distance. "We've been thinking of that. But enough about the revolution. You need to work on those bees. Go find your own place by the river and whisper to them until you feel their hum in your very bones."

I nodded.

"And Aella?" he added.

"Yes?"

"I've never lost an apprentice. Never had one die on me or fail to meet their potential. I won't let you down either."

"Thank you," I said, oddly touched by his words. We shared a smile and then I turned back to the river and made my way to a sunny spot in the rushes to whisper to bees. Which felt utterly ridiculous. Out there along the trail, my father lay under a cairn of rocks. Farther into the Far Reaches, my mother's bones lay under a similar cairn. Beyond her, my family battled the Forbidding, fighting their way out of the vice of evil called the

Empire of War and Wings. And here I was, whispering to bees.

I could hear their hum in my mind and as I closed my eyes and concentrated on it, I could feel them out there, some binding Ivo's ribs together, others deep in the belly of Juste Montpetit, weaving honeycomb to patch his organs and veins. I shivered and they shivered with me. I whispered to them, and they seemed to whisper back.

But the darkness was almost too much for me. Little memories of what I had experienced in the agony of the Cobra Temple kept bursting back and threaded through them were emotions and memories of things I didn't even remember from the experience. Things people had seen or done. I trembled as I remembered plunging a knife into my own belly.

My eyes shot open. A buzzing filled them, and I grasped for the single bee floating around me, reaching for it. It landed on my palm as my tears flowed fast and hard.

"Hold onto me," I whispered. "This is all too much."

Like breaking open a beaver's dam, emotions flooded over me – the crushing weight of my father's death and fear for my siblings and over it all a deep, heavy sense of responsibility, as if by choosing to fight for this land and the people on it, I had chosen to bear the grief of it, but also the responsibility of it. Because if we took this land for ourselves, we would be taking it not just from the Empire but also from the people who had owned it before the Empire arrived.

I'd been born here in Far Stones. I'd lived my sixteen years here. I knew no other home. But the memories I had now showed me a time when my kind was not here. And I was having trouble sorting out how I felt about that.

I didn't realize I was shaking until someone whistled a two-note tune. I spun around to see Osprey standing behind me, leaning against a willow and chewing his toothpick thoughtfully. There was sweat on his brow as he clung to the willow. Was the belly wound getting worse?

"What happened with that snake? They hurt you somehow, but there are no marks."

"They gave me memories."

"Of what?"

I shook my head. "Of everything. They come back slowly …"

He swallowed. "Maybe you can use them to help the Single Wing. If you think of something that can help – anything – tell it to Ivo." He cleared his throat. "Not me, okay? Don't tell me." I tilted my head to the side and his smile was rueful. "I can only be trusted with so much."

He stepped forward, flexing a fist and then opening it – as if he wanted to do something and was holding himself back. "I know everything is murky now, but I need you to know that I would never willingly harm you. I'm doing everything I can to protect you."

"Because I'm the figurehead you need for the revolution," I said, nodding.

He made a sound in his throat and looked away, flushing, as if there was more he wanted to say. I opened my mouth to goad him into saying it, but a sharp sound cracked in the forest behind us and a horn blew.

Our eyes met and then we were scrambling through the reeds and willows to get back to the riverbank.

CHAPTER TWELVE

We reached the fire, breathless and flushed, joining Ivo and a nervous-looking Zayana just before the reeds parted and a pair of masked figures slipped into the clear circle around the fire. They moved with surprising stealth and grace and I couldn't help how my mind saw them and immediately thought, 'snake.'

The two warriors parted, fanning out as a stream of them moved to surround us. Was it my imagination, or were they looking at me a little more than the others? It was hard to tell with the masks, but the back of my neck prickled from the attention. What, exactly, did they expect to see? Had they thought I would be more damaged by the ceremony in the temple?

"Make way for the Adder, the glorious one, he who comes from the belly of the earth."

As if Juste Montpetit needed more titles.

He was being carried on a litter with Ixtap between six masked bearers. The litter was carved in whitewood – every bit of it made to look like snakes woven into a round platform or curling out in long poles to stretch over the shoulders of the bearers.

They set the litter down with care. Juste Montpetit's face was wan and slick with sweat. He kept an arm wrapped around his belly even as he clasped arms with Ixtap in a friendly gesture. Ixtap leaned forward.

"Like this," he said, as his snake manifested, pouring from his mouth and wrapped around Juste's neck. Our crown prince imitated him and my stomach flipped, nausea rising in my throat. Everything about the snakes made me ill. And the strange customs surrounding them did not help with that feeling.

"I shall return when I am ready to ascend," Juste Montpetit said as if making a proclamation. He held his head high, his lovely curls gleaming in the bright sunlight and his large eyes sparkling innocently with them. "We shall forge a great peace between our peoples, made of mutual respect and admiration."

I didn't quite snort, but by the way Ixtap's face twisted, I felt like he was about to. Whatever Juste Montpetit said, he bore no love for the Winged Empire. A burst of memory flooded my mind – thoughts of warning children against birds, looking on the sky as a curse, the tumultuous change of it a threat. Only under the ground was life safe.

I shook my head against someone else's memory and shoved it aside. It was as if my enemy had slid into my mind, changing up to down in a moment. It made my skin crawl. And this was what was supposed to happen to Juste Montpetit. It would have tied him to them even tighter. It could have made him their creature.

"You are our prophesied heir, the one who will lead us to victory and return us to the ways of the ancestors," Ixtap said. "We will wait for you. We bind your people now to silence. They may not speak of us."

I felt a clenching around my throat. Panic bubbled up as I clawed at my neck, but it was gone as quickly as it came. My eyes met Zayana's at the same moment that a snake manifestation fell from her neck and she drew in a gasping breath. Had they really used magic to silence us? I despised these people more every moment.

"There is strength in silencing lies," Ixtap said.

Juste Montpetit nodded. "We are committed to speaking the truth about peace and justice. My people will not deviate from that."

What did that mean to him? His tone sounded like he was agreeing with Ixtap but if he was really committed to truth, he wouldn't silence us from speaking about what we saw. I was growing frustrated by how his words never matched his meaning.

"Keep the sacrifice within your grasp," Ixtap said, nodding to me. "You may find you need more from her."

Juste Montpetit grunted, hunching slightly over his belly. "Have no fear, Ixtap. I have great respect for those I own."

How did you respect someone if you claimed to own them? I could feel my face growing hard. Ivo caught my eyes, shaking his head in warning so fractionally that I barely saw it. But he was right. We were outnumbered. Our fight would have to come later.

My vision flickered as a memory surfaced from those somehow given me by the snake people. A memory of a woman, eyes white and glassy as she whispered, "One will come to lead, but not the one who sees. One will come for memory and one for ambition. One will take the honor and one the price. But both are bound together."

I shivered.

Some of my bees in Juste's belly soared out, spinning through the air to join me, gathering around my head in a cloud. Juste

Montpetit frowned, his upper lip curling in a way that worried me, but he only bowed politely to Ixtap who bowed back, making that 'S' sign in front of him again.

"Until all is accomplished," Le Majest said, turning grandly to us. "Prepare the boat. We leave at once."

Even Zayana looked worried as we gathered the few things we had, put them in the boat, and silently readied it for launch under the hostile gazes of our enemies.

Osprey caught my eye as he readied the boat to launch. He was just as hunched as Juste but he winked at me. Cold crept up my spine at the sight of that. He only ever winked when something bad was happening.

"We situated your boat past the falls," Ixtap said. "From here, there are only a few rapids and then you will reach the sea."

"Eyes forward!" Juste Montpetit barked.

We turned, looking down the river, but something in me rebelled. They were planning something – I could tell. Something that couldn't possibly be good for me or for the revolution. If only I had a way to keep an eye on them – to spy on them.

As I thought of it, a tiny bee began to buzz, walking slowly down my arm.

Was she offering to go with them?

"Fly," I whispered. "Wait patiently with him. Be the eyes of the hive and the ears of the swarm."

She buzzed away. I had no idea how she would be able to get any kind of information for us, but I could feel her buzz apart from the others. It was bright and confident. She did not share my fears.

We were miles downriver before anyone dared to speak. Juste Montpetit sat in the middle of the boat, silently staring out at the shore as the boat floated down the river. The Forbidding tangled along the coast once again and his smile was spooky as he regarded it, his hands tangling round and round a small glowing snake in his lap.

I swallowed down bile more than once as I kept to the prow of the boat, using my pole to keep the nose of the boat off of rocks when it got shallow and away from the slower parts of the river, staying in the fast-moving channel at the center.

"We shall find fast allies with the Hissan people," Juste Montpetit said. "They feel as I do about the need for peace and justice for all."

Wing Ivo cleared his throat. "Had they no healers, Le Majest? I had hoped they could help you."

Juste Montpetit ran a hand idly through his hair as if he wasn't hunched over himself. "They see weakness in consulting healers. They are certain I will shake this poison on my own. I agree."

"A lesser man would be dead already, Le Majest." Wing Ivo's warning was careful. And what he must have meant was that even with my bees, we were running out of time. Even I could see that as Osprey swayed slightly at the tiller. He was showing more signs of this, which meant Le'Majest was getting worse. If we didn't find a healer quickly, he might die. And then I would die, too.

"The Hissan would not have let me leave if they believed that. Their future is pinned to me alongside the future of the Winged Empire."

I bit my lip at his words. Was it all an act? I thought so, but what if I was wrong? What if under all of that, he thought he was doing what was right? What if he really thought he was bringing peace to the Empire? I should try to warn him, shouldn't I?

"I saw things in that ceremony," I said, turning to face him.

"What things did you think you saw?" There was a warning in his voice. But I had to try just once, didn't I?

"They are not friends to the Winged Empire," I said, as certain of that as of anything I ever knew. Behind him, Osprey was shaking his head at me, eyes wide. But, I had to try. I couldn't let this happen without at least warning him. "The things I saw … they have a Wing imprisoned in their territory. A man with two ravens as manifestations. Did they tell you that?"

Behind him, Ivo's jaw dropped. He and Osprey shared a sharp look before making their faces like stone again.

"They hate everything that flies," I pushed on. "Hate the Winged Empire with all their hearts. They will destroy your Empire if they can. They will kill your father if they can. It's all they've wanted for generations."

Juste Montpetit's expression never wavered. His wide eyes stayed innocent and his smile smooth.

"Nonsense. You're only a foolish girl with the wrong kind of magic. These people are one with us in peace. We shall meet the commitments I have given them with integrity and dignity."

A creeping sense came over me. What commitments had he made?

I made the sign of the bird respectfully, eyes lowered. I shouldn't have spoken. He wasn't ready to hear it. But if he didn't listen, then how many people would die when the Hissan people finally got the revenge they wanted and rolled over the freshly-unarmed Winged Empire like a flood?

I was still bowed when a hand grabbed my hair.

Juste Montpetit moved with the speed of a snake. He wrenched my head back, looking into my eyes.

"The next time you utter what you think you saw, you pathetic colonial, I will cut one of those pretty eyes right from your face. Do you understand me?" His smile never wavered. His glorious curls didn't even dislodge.

"Le Majest." I met his eyes without allowing the spike of terror within me to show. It was all I would give him – an acknowledgment of his position.

"I want to hear agreement," he hissed.

"And I want my freedom," I returned. "We all want things we can't have."

"Osprey," Juste Montpetit said the name like a caress. A wicked gleam danced in his bright eyes. "Take hold of this bee-lover."

I looked past Juste Montpetit to see Osprey close his eyes for a heartbeat, biting his lip. Ivo jabbed him in the ribs hard enough that his eyes snapped open and his expression turned to stone as he strode forward.

"Keep the tiller firmly in hand, Wing Ivo," Juste Montpetit said as the boat wavered in the river. "This does not concern you. Move even an inch and I will have Osprey hit you. Move more and I'll have him slit your throat. I have plenty of Wings."

"She's my apprentice," Ivo said calmly. "I would prefer her alive."

"So would I," the crown prince said. "But, like she said, we all want things we can't have."

Osprey stepped carefully around the crown prince and Zayana – who was scrambling backward quickly to join Ivo in the stern – and took up a place beside me, carefully taking my waist in his hands. He was so near that I could smell him. His scent reminded me of cloves.

Juste Montpetit smirked, "Shove her head under the water until I say you may stop."

Osprey froze. I shot a panicked look at his eyes and saw my fear mirrored. There. A sharp stab of ice tore through me. His hand on my waist was trembling.

"That was a direct order," Juste whispered. "Or have you stopped snivelling every time I send you a little casket."

What could he mean by – Osprey moved so fast that I barely had time to suck in a deep breath before my head was underwater, my eyes bulging open as I fought against his hold. He held me by the back of the head – not the hair – and had a hand pressed between my shoulders, holding my upper body against the gunwale of the boat.

I hadn't thought he would do that. I'd thought – based on that look, based on all he'd said – that he'd fight for me.

I bucked against his grip, but the way he held me kept me completely immobilized without giving me enough space to even fight him. Terror rose inside me. I fought against it, trying to remember that I must not breathe in water. Panicking would only speed the need for breath. A tiny part of me realized that the way Osprey held me was keeping the rest of my body from damage, but it was impossible to be grateful as my lungs began to burn, fire shooting from them through my body and searing my mind.

I couldn't breathe. I needed air.

My hands hit the sides of the boat uselessly.

Fear filled me.

Long moments passed, and passed, and passed until stars danced across the green of the water and my vision flickered.

Relentless. Do not surrender.

Without my permission, my lungs opened and I sucked in a breath of water. Agonizing pain filled me. Conscious thought ended. And it was nothing but pain and more pain and the buzz of my bees echoing endlessly in my mind.

Everything went black.

CHAPTER THIRTEEN

I blacked out a lot around Juste Montpetit.

I awoke, puking water and coughing, my lungs on fire, my consciousness a ghost of a thing I could barely keep from slipping through my fingers.

"Enough," Juste Montpetit ordered in a weak voice. "She's seen enough of your attentions, Guardian. Return to the stern of the boat."

Osprey's anguished eyes met mine and though his face remained stony, his eyes seemed as if they were begging my forgiveness. He steadied me with gentle hands, his lips parting as his head shook faintly. I could see the words forming on his lips, see the air breathing across them as he tried to find the right ones. His face had a streak of dirt running across it and his lip was bloody. I must have managed a lucky shot after all. I was too drowned to do more than lift my head.

"I said, release her." Juste's words were steely. "Or must I remind you again who gives the orders and who carries them out."

Osprey let go of me like he was dropping something hot, shame burning bright across his face. He was flushed, his nostrils flaring with every breath and his fists shaking. He was on the verge of something, but I didn't know if it was fighting or sobbing. Refusing to meet my eyes, he stalked to the stern of the boat, still shaking from head to foot.

"You don't dare do that again, Le Majest," Wing Ivo said carefully. He had a bruise on his cheek. When had he gotten that? He rubbed it unconsciously. "Please, don't risk yourself. Her bees must hold you together until a healer can be found."

"Only because she stabbed me in the first place," the crown prince said grimly. I lifted my head just enough to see him situating himself in the floor of the boat, hands clasped to his belly and red blood again staining his shirt. My bees hummed happily in the wound, working to mend him even as my strength slowly rose again.

Zayana hurried to his side, already reaching for her belt pouch.

I wheezed as I pushed myself to my wobbling feet, looking down on him with fury in my eyes.

"Let that be a lesson to you, bees," he snarled. "You do not defy me. You do not dare defy me or I will make you suffer a hundred times without killing you. I will burn you with fire and skewer you with blades, I will crush your bones, and I will steal your breath. I will make you wish your heart would break to save you from the agony of all I will do to you and I will make those you *think* care about you be the instruments of your torture. And I will love every second of it as I slowly choke out your life."

My knees were shaking, my hands with them. But I would not let him break me. I met his eyes, refusing to look away, refusing to be beaten.

"Do you understand me this time?" he asked. Which was the wrong question, because understanding someone was not acquiescing to them.

"Absolutely, I do."

I was proud of how my voice didn't waver. Even prouder of how I was able to walk straight-backed to the bow of the boat, pick up my pole, and resume my position fending us off of the rocks in the roiling river. I did not look back again all day. Not even when Zayana offered me water and fish. Not even when she whispered desperately that I could eat, that Le Majest was sleeping. That she'd seen a pink lotus flower growing in the water and that meant peace. Not even when the sun dipped low and darkness swallowed us and the only light to see by was the light of our manifestations.

After a moment, Os flew low over my head, darting over the boat and out in front of us, lighting the river with purplish-white light. It was a moment before I realized his rider was on his back. A sharp pain shot through me, but I refused to think of what that might mean and what part he'd had in hurting me.

I could hear him cursing to himself fainter and fainter as he flew away. If words could slay, an army would fall before him.

Our boat was bathed in a light golden glow and when I looked up, Harpy flapped above us, in perfect time with the speed of the boat.

I glanced back, swallowing as I saw Zayana and the crown prince curled in separate spots in the hull, their breathing easy as they slept. Behind them, Ivo steered the boat, his back still straight despite hours of doing the same. I opened my mouth to speak, but he shook his head. Probably wise. No point in waking those who would harm me.

"We'll run," he mouthed to me. A promise that he probably couldn't keep, but I was grateful all the same. No one else was offering to risk themselves for me.

I fixed my mouth into a grim line and faced forward again. I probably could have slept, but I felt no desire to let my guard down. Every bit of me tingled in anticipation as I waited for the next attack, the next pain, the next reminder that my life was no longer my own.

We traveled for hours into the night as the warmth bled from the earth into the cooling air and goosebumps rose along my arms and every place that my torn clothing exposed my skin to the air. I ached everywhere, inside and out. My heart ached most of all.

I was so tired, so shoved to the edge of myself that I was seeing visions. Little flashes of forest and Forbidding kept filling my vision. I blinked rapidly the first time and it disappeared immediately, but after it happened three more times, I started to get a headache. Almost drowning wasn't good for a person.

At long last, a glimmer of gold appeared on the horizon. Dawn.

But it was not dawn. The glow was more muted, more faint. And as we drifted closer and closer, I realized what I was seeing. The port. Karkatua. And with it, Juste Montpetit would no longer need my bees and my life would be forfeit. I tensed, wrapping my arms around myself to try to keep from falling apart. I needed a plan and I didn't know where to begin. Because though Ivo was on my side, he wasn't strong enough to stand with me against Juste and Osprey. And while Zayana was sympathetic, she was too weak to help. And while Osprey might see hope in me, he would snuff out that hope in a moment if he was ordered to.

I swallowed down bile as the lights grew closer and brighter.

In the distance, the real sun began to rise, painting the

morning a vivid pink and ultramarine. So beautiful. Perhaps it would be my last dawn. I tried to savor it, staring out into the bright sky and then closing my eyes as I sucked in long breaths of soft dewy air.

I heard the rustle of feathers and then felt a whisper on my neck, as warm and soft as it was hard to hear.

"With all my honor I am laid before you. With the breaking of my grip on the sword, I am prostrate. With my still-beating heart presented, I am at your mercy." Osprey's voice was thick with sorrow.

"Where did you learn those words," I whispered back, eyes still fixed on the dawn.

"They were the words offered by Illui King of the Citrine Islands when he offered his swords in surrender to the Winged Empire." His voice was hoarse.

"And what happened to him?" I asked.

"They beheaded him."

"Perhaps I will do the same," I said icily.

"That is your choice," he whispered, his breath hot on my neck, and then he was gone.

I spun, looking for him, and saw him in the stern of the boat, whispering with Ivo. Osprey's eyes were puffy and red. Ivo shook his head, pointing to where Zayana and Le Majest remained asleep in the hull of the boat. Osprey leaned forward, his body language more insistent and then Ivo glanced at me and sighed.

Osprey stepped back again, making the sign of the bird and then Os popped into existence beside him, a bright flare of purplish-white light. His manifestor leapt onto his back, soaring toward me. I barely had time to gasp before he swept me up in his arms, drawing me tight against him.

"One more time, House Apidae. You vowed to fight alongside me. I am asking that you let me show you something that will help. One last flight and then I shall let you go to fly free with Ivo until my binding forces me to hunt you down."

We swept up into the air, speeding over the flashing river and toward the city. Furtively, I rubbed the armband he'd given me. That feather would come in very handy if he did end up tracking me. I would know when he was close. I peeked at the feather. It glowed bright and hot.

"What are you going to show me?" I asked warily.

My lungs still ached even as they breathed in the fecund algae scent of the river. My body felt like exhausted jelly. I was still getting frustrating flashes of painful memories from my torture in the Cobra Temple and those headache-inducing momentary visions were still disorienting me.

As we neared the walls of Karkatua, a memory flashed over me – the man with two ravens stood on the hill where Karkatua stood now. He pointed toward where I was and his ravens shot out like arrows, a flock of other birds following. Behind them, Claws roared, their polearms held high, their feet churning up the swampy grass as they charged.

I swallowed. He'd been a general. And they put him in that tower.

I shook the memory away.

"It will help with hope. Help with knowing why we are sacrificing everything for this."

"Why you might be willing to drown me in a river?" I asked.

His body froze. His words dripped with sorrow.

"Why we must both do whatever we must to make this real. Because our blood can hold back something worse than the Forbidding. Our pain can save our people."

"And what is worse than the Forbidding?" I breathed.

"The evil of man. The tangles of his pride and power. The insidious creeping of his lust to take and take and take."

"And more specifically?"

"Have you heard of a place called Canaht?"

I shuddered.

"By your reaction, I know that you have. I was twelve when they brought those children to my estates. I watched them slay little ones with big tearful eyes clutching little blankets or sock toys in their chubby hands. Three they killed right in front of me and then I was given the rest to 'manage' as my father left again on campaign. I held their hands. I prayed with them in the dark of night. But any time I failed to please, one was taken from me. Taken and killed in front of me. And when I was named Osprey, they bound me with magic. If I defy an order, another dies that very moment. I feel it in the symbol they embedded in my chest. I feel each death like it is my own – only its worse, because I still live as they perish. Every one of them who dies in fear and terror without someone to hold them is my fault. What else could be enough to bind me? What else would lead me to plunge your head underwater until you nearly drowned? What would make me stand quietly as they tortured your father? I am bound by ties unseen and if I take my own life to be free of the burden, it will kill them all. So, tell me again that you hate me, House Apidae, but don't expect it to matter. I already hate myself more than you ever could. I'm already cloaked in shame and winnowed by guilt.

Nothing can wash it away. It sticks to me like tar. It blackens my heart and everything I touch."

I gasped, twisting in his grip to stare at him with my mouth open.

His expression was bare to me. I could see through it to the torment seated in his soul. And yet his hands held me gently.

"The Empire of War and Wings will never stop. It will never cease until it has crushed us all," he whispered. "That's what I want to show you. And I want to show you that you aren't alone in fighting it. There is still hope for you. Tomorrow, when Ivo takes you away, he isn't going to tell me where you are going. I vowed to try to protect you as much as I could. I plan to protect you from myself. It will be hard for me to track you if I don't know where you're going. Hard for me to betray you. I want you to fly free." He tapped the leather cuff of his that I still wore. "I want you to be the symbol the people need to offer their blood for freedom, just as you and I offer ours."

I couldn't hate him anymore. Not now that I knew. I couldn't see him as anything but someone bent under an impossible burden fighting so hard to bear it.

The walls of Karkatua cast a long shadow over us. I swallowed, overwhelmed by the need to show him everything I was feeling. I licked my lips, hesitating, and then – grasping all my courage – I leaned in to kiss him. He pulled back, a single finger to my lips.

He cleared his throat, looking away with a sharp wince. "Not today, House Apidae. Not like this. Not when I almost took your life today."

He flinched as he said it.

"Why not?" I asked, my cheeks flushing. If he was right and

we were both only going to live a short time, what did it matter if I kissed him? What did it matter if I tried to show him that I didn't see him as shameful and evil – not even after he'd almost killed me.

I reached for his hand and he let me take it, but he looked away, turning his cheek to me and his face away.

He let out a shuddering breath. "I can't even look at you. Don't cut me deeper than I already bleed. I beg you."

I swallowed and nodded but I held onto that hand as we reached the gates. He stepped off of Os's back, drawing me after him.

"Let's go eat apple pielets and drink clover ale," he said lightly as if nothing of significance had passed between us.

I swallowed back the tears that threatened to burst over me like storm clouds. This world – this harsh horrible world – was too much for me. But I would not let it remain like this. I would be relentless.

BOOK TWO: INTO THE NEST

Blossom soft, petal bright,

Bathe in sun, drink in light,

Sing the charming thrum of grow,

Let the rainbow colors flow,

Buzz, buzz, hum, hum,

We the bees, we the drum.

Our rhythm makes the flowers rise,

Our melody fills the skies.

- Forgotten Folk Song

CHAPTER FOURTEEN

Osprey led me into Karkatua. I would have been lost if I'd entered on my own. I'd only been here twice before and it had been many years. While I remembered the huge totems on either side of the city gate – eagles here to show strength and courage – I didn't remember much else and the grandeur of the city surprised me. The guards on either side of the totems were Claws, dressed in the finely embroidered jackets of their order – a darker blue than those Swan Claws who had accompanied Juste Montpetit. They demanded Osprey give his name and mine for the ledger before allowing us in the city, frowning at our torn and stained clothing.

"We've heard nothing of late from Vlaren or Portua Town," one of the Claws said. "Do you have word from your travels?"

"With reluctance, I must pass on the news that Vlaren has been lost to the Forbidding," Osprey said, shoving one of his picks between his teeth. He didn't touch me, but he kept himself slightly in front of me as if he was protecting me – or maybe hiding me – from the Claws.

The guard cursed grimly but he let us pass.

"Before anything else, we need clothing. We stand out in these rags," Osprey said, flicking the tattered embroidery on the sleeve of his jacket.

"I have no coin," I said, feeling suddenly very ragged as I watched people already beginning their days, their clothing tidy and clean.

"Allow me one last gift, House Apidae," he said, maneuvering me into an alley and then to the back of a shop there.

It stood on tall stilts worked with bird feathers and claws carved into them and Osprey led me up a winding, narrow spiral staircase to a tall walkway between two roofs. A tiny, perfectly round, door – just large enough to allow us to crawl through – was set in the belly of a carved white-wood owl, its wings cupped around the door and its head carved cocked to the side as if it was considering us suspiciously.

Osprey pulled out his belt pouch, removed a tiny brass key, and opened the door.

I wanted to follow him but the sight of the city below took my breath away. Smoke curled up from the chimneys, slender twists in the cool of the morning. The pink of dawn had faded into the jasmine of early morning, lifting up a scent fresh and bright over the cedar-shingled roofs and tall house totems that filled Karkatua. The city walls were set in rock and stone, with birds carved on every square inch by hands that varied from juvenile to master as if the citizens themselves had taken to carving their totems into the walls. Bright banners snapped in the wind and as the city rolled out toward the sea the bright sapphire of it kissed the sky in a molten haze, flashing water meeting pale expanse like two entangled lovers.

My breath caught in my lungs at the sight.

"It's very like my home," Osprey said, clearing his throat. He wiped sweat from his forehead with the back of his sleeve. He was getting worse. "Which is why I let this room. Come on. We have little time before Le Majest awakens and notices us."

Reluctantly, I followed him into the tiny round door.

I'd expected to be disappointed after the beauty of the city from the rooftops, but instead, I paused within the door, surprised by the sight of the place. It was a garret. The beams supporting the roof were fully exposed and met the floor on either side. Opposite the round door, was a round window of equal size, lighting the small airy room. Someone – likely the person I had followed into this place – had carved ospreys in flight on every available surface, marching up the roof beams, soaring across the floor, over and under the window, wingtips meeting. It was like a song dedicated to the seabird. A heap of cloth and blankets and mismatched pillows in one corner – messy and lived in – was clearly his bed. And to the other side was a low bench covered in scattered items. One boot. A notebook half-filled. Spilled ink. A length of bottle-green silk.

I looked to Osprey whose expression was suddenly nervous as he bit at the pick in his mouth.

"Well, don't stay hovering at the door. Let's find you some new clothing."

"You keep women's clothing in your rooms?" I asked.

He snorted. "Make yourself at home and wait one moment for me."

He slipped behind a silk screen, dyed black and stitched with silver ospreys. His jacket flew over the side of it, sending the screen rocking. Then his ruined down-trimmed shirt. Then the trousers. By then, I was blushing but in moments he stepped out, in his trousers and boots, buttoning a feather-lined shirt. I could see the glowing feather peeking through where it was laid over his heart, the muscles of his body were hard and flat as if to show the difference between he rest of him and that one odd, upraised spot.

I studied his torso, thinking about that feather. How had they put it within his skin? And more importantly, could it be taken out?

He looked up, color washing across his cheeks. "I suppose there's no need to keep it hidden from you, since you know it's there."

He grabbed a fresh jacket from a chair and slipped it over the shirt, adjusting the cuffs of his dark jacket as he pulled osprey-feather edging from the sleeves.

"Never mind," I teased. "I see that you do have women's clothing here."

He gave me one of those savage winks again. "Tease all you want. If you dress well, people listen. And these days, I need all the hearts I can sway."

I felt my cheeks heating again. In those tight black trousers and sharply tailored dark jacket, he'd be more than able to steal hearts.

"Come on," he said, walking to one corner and opening a trap door. He led me down a narrow, windowless set of stairs to the shop below – a shop, I realized that was a tailor's shop. "This is where we'll find what you need."

He snatched up a pair of dark trousers and boots, eyeing me and then the clothing and then me again, before shoving them at me. A linen shirt was next, cut in a way I'd never seen before and then a sharp-collared short-jacket just like the ones I'd seen on Wings before, but this one was a rich red with yellow trim.

"Yellow for bees," he said as he handed it to me. It had brass buttons trimming the edge and I felt my face heating just looking at it.

"It's too fine," I said awkwardly. "I could never afford it."

"I told you it was a gift."

"This is a tailor shop!" I objected. "These are their wares!"

"How shocking. And here I thought it was a cheesemonger's shop."

"Osprey!"

He rolled his eyes at me. "House Apidae, I will compensate the owner of the shop. Now, hurry up the stairs and get dressed. I have more to show you and I need you dressed properly before I can. Eventually, the crown prince will awaken, and he will want to know where we are. Do you wish to miss this last opportunity for me to show you something beautiful instead of always the horrible?"

"No," I admitted.

"Then hurry up."

I raced up the stairs, ducked behind his screen, and began to strip off my soiled clothing. Something filmy and black sailed over the screen.

"More clothing?" I asked before I realized what they were and my cheeks burned hot. He'd given me fresh underthings.

I dressed hurriedly, feeling cleaner the moment my old clothing was off and the new began to replace them. I had stitches in a few places. I gave them a quick look as I dressed. Nothing was puffy or red. No infection. They still pulled and pinched as I tried to move, but what did I expect? I was tugging on the boots before I had time to catch my breath, amazed at how well all the clothing fit me. But maybe I shouldn't be. After all, Osprey spent enough time watching me. He should at least be able to guess my size after all of that.

I stepped out from behind the screen, buttoning my jacket and looked up to find Osprey there, staring yet again. He held out a comb in his hand, strangely still. Not even his toothpick moved.

"I can't use combs," I said. "My hair is too thick."

I reached up self-consciously to run my hands through my hair, little bits of leaves and debris came out of my hair as I did that, but my thick curls remained.

Osprey seemed to recover himself. He gave me a small key. "This is for you. If you need this place – for anything – you know where it is. It's yours to use if you need it." He cleared his throat awkwardly. "Whatever comes next – remember this. That you have a safe spot and that you stopped here for just a moment and that moment was beautiful."

His smile was sad as he jammed yet another of his endless supply of toothpicks into his mouth.

"Where do you get those things?" I asked awkwardly, not sure what to do about the key.

"I whittle. Helps the nerves."

"You can't possibly carve enough f them for your habit."

"I do the impossible daily."

And then he was turning and leading me back out the little round door from this little temporary safety and back into the unknown.

CHAPTER FIFTEEN

He led me down the winding staircase out into the small city as the first drops of rain began to fall from the sky. I looked up with a sense of foreboding. Where a bright morning sky had been only minutes before, dark clouds were gathering overhead.

"I should have grabbed cloaks, too," Osprey said, worry lining his forehead.

He was surprisingly solicitous as he led me through the winding streets of Karatua, holding out. The city was waking up, where there had been only a few people when we arrived, there were now larger groups. Street vendors opened their carts, lifting fabric shades to reveal leather belts tooled with a variety of bird motifs, or juicy fruits, frying cakes, or sleek leather hats with wide brims – the newest fashion of Far Stones. Osprey snatched one up from a vendor, flipping him a silver coin as he jammed it on his head without missing a step. The man called a thank you and we moved on.

He'd been right about our clothing. We blended in with ease – shockingly. I hadn't realized that Karkatua was so much richer than Far Reach. Finely embroidered jackets were seen everywhere, and people even wore tooled belts with gilding over the buckles. Most of them had a bright, unworn patch where a scabbard used to be – empty now.

But it was their eyes that shocked me. I was used to the bluff, honest looks of Far Stones. We prided ourselves that we could take the measure of a man with a single glance – and we measured everyone. But today the faces I passed were hardened and guarded. As we passed one of the squares, I saw why.

A ring of Swan Claws was stationed around a platform at the center of the square – at least a dozen of them with pikes in hand. Between them, glowing braziers burned – likely to light the square at night or to warm the guards. Behind their ring, under the rough wooden platform, a variety of knives and swords had been piled – taken from the citizenry no doubt. But what was worse was the display on the platform.

There were five of them. Or at least, there had *been* five of them.

Five men in stocks, faces drawn and pale, eyes removed. I sucked in a hiss of breath, remembering my father like that. I could barely hold back tears and my body shuddered in response.

Two of the men were dead already, slumped in the stocks with flies buzzing over them, flesh already hanging from bones. The other three looked close to death.

Beneath them, painted in careful, beautiful script surrounded by scrollwork were the words.

Speech shall be peaceable and lovely. Tongues that speak harsh prejudice will be removed. Eyes that cannot see the truth will be removed.

I couldn't look away. I couldn't stop the shaking in my hands and feet. I tried to take a step, but my leaden feet rebelled. These people deserved to be seen. To be remembered.

Osprey's hand found my upper arm, pulling me roughly to him and forcing my heavy feet to walk past and dip into an alley.

"Get a hold of yourself or you'll draw attention," he whispered, toothpick bobbing wildly.

I sucked in a long breath. "Did you see that? Those men are disfigured and rotting because they *said* something the Empire didn't like. Words, Osprey. They took their eyes and tongues for words!"

"Shhhh!" he hissed, glancing behind him and frogmarching me further down the alley and around a turn to a spot that squeezed between two buildings so narrowly that we could barely face each other. It smelled like rotten fruit and chamber pots.

"That's what we're fighting, House Apidae. That's why. But you can't go saying that where people can hear you."

I couldn't stop the shaking. Shivers ran up and down me, making me useless. Come on, Aella! Don't let this overwhelm you!

"I want to fight right now, Osprey. Why are we waiting? Why can't I just bring down my bees and you leap on your Osprey and we go! If I remove the bees before you get back, Juste Montpetit won't be able to say a word of command to you. And I'll just tie you up here in this alley and then the children won't be harmed." I was pleading, tears tracking down my face as the rain picked up outside the narrow alley. "And then they won't be taking any more eyes or tongues or anything else. Those are people's fathers and brothers and sons! And they disfigured them and killed them like they did to my father – my old man who made me my little bow and taught me to shoot it, who carved little birds for me and taught me to ride wild horses – *my* father. And they left them to rot like they would have left him."

The buzzing in my head was almost uncontrollable. I could feel bees bubbling up inside me, desperate to release.

"Shhh," Osprey said, and he leaned his shaking forehead against mine, pinning me against the rough wall behind me with both hands on my upper arms. "Shhh. Calm down."

"I see *that* and you want me to *calm down*?" I felt like I was going to fly apart in every direction. "Why do they let it happen? Why is no one rising up against this?"

"Good," he said firmly. "Ask the right questions. Why do you think they aren't fighting? Stop being ruled by emotion and answer that question – and trust me, it's not because those poor wretches are more dear to you than they are to them."

"They aren't doing anything because their weapons were stolen and they feel powerless. Something that *you* helped with!"

He flinched but he didn't remove his hands or his forehead from mine. He spoke in a fierce whisper.

"Maybe that's true for some people, House Apidae, but not for all of them. Some people want to fight. But what can you do if it's just you running in there, even with your prodigious bees? Hmm? Could you take out all those Claws guarding those men yourself? And then what? How will you get them somewhere safe? What will you do when reinforcements arrive from the barracks or the gates? What if you're so lucky that you manage to defeat them? And you know you won't. You're just one girl. You'll be overwhelmed in minutes. But even if you did it, then you have one city in rebellion. One. Your supplies cut off. Winged Empire ships sailing toward you full of Claws and Wings ready to rip your heart out and feast on it. No plan for what comes next. No supplies. No fortifications."

"But I have to fight!" I sniffed back my tears, forcing myself to calm down. Even if he was right, I refused to surrender. "Why make me vow to join you if you weren't going to fight?"

"I am going to fight, House Apidae. We all are," he said, voice shaking now as if emotions were overcoming him, too. "But we're going to be smart about it. We're going to set up proper supply chains and a militia and have people ready with their tasks already in mind before we raise the flag and start this. We're going to find a proper general to lead the action and we're going to have a Forbidding-taken plan instead of going off on a rampage like a carabao in heat. Do you understand that?"

"Yes," I whispered.

"You can do this, House Apidae," he whispered, his forehead warm against mine. "You're tough enough to survive giant snakes in the jungle. You're tough enough to survive your father's murder. You're tough enough to survive nearly being drowned." His voice broke slightly there. "You can withstand this, too."

He pulled back, though there was still barely inches between us in the tight alley.

"Why did you bring me to see this?" I asked, lip trembling, arms wrapping themselves around me protectively.

"That wasn't that I was bringing you to see," he said quietly, his toothpick bobbing wildly again as he chewed the life out of it.

He pulled a lacey handkerchief from his sleeve – the same one from his pack, I thought, and – looking awkward, his eyes full of some emotion that was close to pain, he dabbed at my tears before offering the handkerchief to me. I shook my head. He should keep it – whoever it was from.

"Lace," I said, offering him a slight smile. "What would the lady who gave you that think of you standing here right now?"

He swallowed and a look of nervousness passed over his face. “Skies only know.”

So, there *was* a lady.

I swallowed, too, feeling foolish suddenly. No wonder he’d turned my kiss away.

You have bigger thigs to worry about, Aella. Keep your head together.

“Let’s go see that solution,” I said, raising my chin defiantly. I would not be a fool girl. I had a fight to win against the biggest empire in history and I didn’t have time to be distracted.

“As you say,” he agreed, slipping back out of the alley into the pouring rain.

So, why did I feel so disappointed to leave this stinking alley with him?

Chapter Sixteen

He worked his way through back alleys, avoiding the main squares and streets – likely to spare my feelings, though I looked hungrily at the main streets whenever I got the chance. Karkatua was gorgeous. Tall spires rose through the city with brass wings or birds attached to the tops of the spires. Weathervanes, I thought, or possibly just decoration, but some of the birds would be as large as I was if they were on the ground and they were very elaborately done. Some were polished and bright as the sun and others had aged with green clouding the surface and filling the dips and cracks.

There were totems here, of course. There were bird totems in every town and at every home in the Far Stones, but there were just so many here it was almost like a forest inside the city. Totems stood outside every shop and home, proudly displaying the Bird House of those within or perhaps wishing for wisdom and prosperity. They made me feel at home, like these were my people. And that made what was happening to them hurt even worse.

Finally, we found a blue door that Osprey liked the look of. He paused outside it, leaning against the door as a tremor rocked his lean, muscular body. His dark face was paler than usual, the sweat across his brow was getting more profuse. He pulled a handkerchief from his pocket and mopped his brow.

"Getting worse?" I whispered.

"It comes in waves." He popped a toothpick between his lips instead and leaned close to me so I could hear his faint whisper. "I want you to watch but to be silent. There are things you need to see but even among our own we must be circumspect."

He waited for me to nod before he opened the door and led me through a dark corridor to an inn common room beyond. We made the sign of the bird politely as we entered the bright room. Windows were opened to the streets beyond and the sounds of hawkers in the streets filled the background behind the clink and clang of breakfast being served hot and steaming to the patrons filling the common room. They conversed quietly together, filling every seat of the wide room. There were sailors in wide-bottomed trousers, farmers in from other towns in Far Stones with the mark of fighting the Forbidding etched into the lines around their eyes, and merchant guards with broken noses and hard eyes. They paid us no mind at all.

The scent of acorn porridge and fresh lavender tea with honey made my stomach rumble, but Osprey didn't stop, leading me instead through another door to a tiny room beyond with its own window and a long bar under the window. There was an assortment of stools under it. Three people hunched over steaming tea at the tiny bar. This window had panes of clouded glass – impossible to see through clearly – but even closed in, they whispered as if afraid of being overheard.

The door squeaked behind us and they looked up in alarm, only sagging in relief when they saw Osprey.

"Forbidding take it, Osprey!" one of them said as he practically deflated with relief.

There were three of them.

Per – a successful fisherman with five boats who had lived in Karkatua all his life and was barely older than my brother Oska. How he'd been so successful so quickly wasn't explained to me and I didn't ask. Judging by his sour expression at the mention of the Empire, I could guess he'd inherited the business. Possibly because his parent or grandparent had been taken from him. He stared intently at his tea, only speaking if he had a sharp point to make and then making it in as few words as possible.

Brielle was a Claw. She wore her uniform like it was a part of her body, but the defiant look in her eyes when my gaze wandered over it told me she didn't want questions asked. She eyed me with suspicion, never taking her eyes from me.

The third was a bulky man in a blacksmith's apron named Ames. He was friendlier, but his gestures were nervous, and he looked often at the door.

They spoke in what appeared to be a code. I couldn't puzzle out what they meant even as I ate the pielets and clover ale that Osprey ordered from the inn's serving girl.

Eventually, Osprey asked me to show one of my bees.

"Show our friends what you have with you, House Apidae," he said tightly, giving me a brief smile when I held out my palm and allowed a single bee to erupt from it.

My bee had a mind of its own, buzzing energetically around the solemn group. They eyed it with wary fear – and then eyed me the same way when it landed on the shell of my ear and stayed there.

"Bees," Brielle said almost as if it was a judgment, but though the others licked their lips nervously, it was hope that I saw in their eyes, not fear. "All we need now is a real general. Don't look at me like that, Osprey. You know you can't lead us. You know that all the roots and channels we've been forming are nothing without someone competent to lead. Ivo is a warrior beyond measure – and there are others like him – but none of them have campaign experience. None of them can lead a real action when the time comes. And we need that, or we will fail. Can you not –"

Osprey cut her off. "No. Don't ask again."

The tension was so thick between them that I scrambled for some way to ease it. "I know of a general."

Osprey shot me a furious look but Brielle squinted with a mocking smile. "You do? Your accent is Far Reach and by your big-eyed looks, I'd say you've rarely left that hay-eared place. What generals do you know?"

"One with two ravens," I said defiantly.

I saw Osprey scrunch his nose with irritation out of the corner of my eye. His toothpick snapped.

Brielle snorted. "Victore? You've been listening to wild stories, girl. The man is long dead. Taken by the Forbidding over a decade ago. If you want to dream dreams, do it on your own time and don't waste mine."

"He's –" I began, but Osprey stepped on my foot. A reminder to be quiet.

"Bees or no bees, she needs tempering, Osprey," Brielle said to him. "I trust we can leave that to you?"

Osprey's eyes glittered with irritation, but I didn't know if that was directed at her or at me. "We all have our roles to play, Brielle."

He was quick to wrap up after that, speaking in their code so rapidly that I couldn't hope to guess the meaning and then handing off a few small missives for them to deliver.

"Soon," he said as he turned to leave. "The dawn comes soon."

Their fierce nods at least agreed on one thing – we all wanted revolution.

CHAPTER SEVENTEEN

We were silent as he led me through the city – by a different route this time. He was likely irritated with me – but I was just as irritated with him. My bee buzzed around my head, showing my displeasure. Why had he silenced me and made me look like a fool to those other people? I wasn't a fool. I'd seen the general taken and imprisoned by the snake people.

At the thought of them, my vision blackened for a moment, and instead of seeing Osprey speed walking down the alley in front of me, I was seeing Ixtap through a shaky, skittering view. He was in a dimly lit room with earthen walls – a tunnel? Arranged in front of him were some of his masked men, their spears held over their heads. Just as quickly as I'd seen them, they were gone.

I staggered, gasping.

Osprey spun around, taking my arm with more irritation than solicitude. "Would you dismiss that bee already? If anyone sees, you'll be the talk of the city and that won't be good for either of us."

"Are you so determined to see me fail?" I hissed.

"What?" he looked genuinely surprised, shaking his head.

"Those people were part of the Single Wing weren't they? And that means I'm supposed to be your symbol to them. But all you did was make me look like a fool."

He raised his eyebrows. "I brought you there to show you off – to let them see that we'd found you and that you're everything we hoped for and instead …" He drew in an irritated breath, trying to control his temper. "If you looked like a fool, it's only because you acted like one. The first thing out of your mouth was a wild theory! You need to learn to think before you speak and act, Aella. I forget how young you are. I forget how little experience you have with anything off your homestead. But this requires careful planning and smooth orchestration."

"And it requires courage. And inspiration," I argued crossing my arms over my chest. I didn't like that he was saying I was too young and too inexperienced. It stung. Hadn't I proved my courage and quick thinking? I would *get* experience. "Which, incidentally, I have! I think I'm going to go find that general and free him and bring him here to help us."

Osprey's jaw clamped shut so fast I heard it click together. He closed his eyes, breathing through his nose as if trying to control his temper.

"You're going to go find someone you think is a general. In a place you've never seen before that could be anywhere in the world. So that you can ask him to lead an army you don't have. On the assumption that he will be on your side and want to fight for you. And you've just told all this to the person most likely to try to stop you." He ran a hand through his hair, his face screwing up in pain for a moment before he whispered to himself. "What are you doing? You really have gone mad. It's put you over the edge."

I didn't care if he wanted to mutter to himself. He couldn't just act like I was a naïve little girl and then be done with the conversation.

"When your fight is gone, you might as well just roll over and die. I still have fight in me, Osprey. I'm not like you. I don't drown people I call my allies. I haven't come to accept my chains."

His eyes snapped open. "What makes you think I have?"

"You never try to get creative. You never try to work around them."

"There are lives on the line," he hissed. "Precious lives. Hundreds of them. I can't afford to be so immature and cavalier as you are."

I felt my cheeks heating. "Yeah, you're so mature and wise, Osprey, holding my head underwater until I nearly drown and then whisking me away as if nothing happened for a tour of this city. Maybe I've never left the Far Stones." I was still stinging from Brielle's comment about my wide eyes. "But lack of experience is something that can be easily changed. Lack of courage can't be. I'm not going to accept an Empire that sentences my family to death and shuts people up by cutting out their tongues and gouging out their eyes!"

He hissed between clenched teeth, looking frantically down the alley in both directions. He ran a hand over his face. "Please, for the love of open skies and fresh air, would you please be quiet before you ruin everything."

I closed my mouth and glared at him. But the glare had guilt in it, too. I might have gone too far. It might not have been prudent to yell all my intentions at him in an alley. I suddenly felt very small.

"I'm going to get you out of here," he said, shaking his head.

"It was a mistake to bring you here. I thought it would help but … you're not ready for this." He shook his head, turning to the wall beside him and hitting it with the palm of his hand – not hard, but as if he was trying to physically release frustration. He hit it again. "We'll get you to Ivo and he'll leave right away. You'll be out of this mess and gone."

"I want to fight. I've been telling you that!" I hated being dismissed like this, as if I somehow wasn't worthy of fighting with him just because I was urging him to action.

"You're too young for this."

"You're barely older than I am!" He wasn't making any sense.

"Exactly." He turned back to me, his face firm as if he had made up his mind. "But I've seen something of the world. I know that courage isn't enough. That good intentions aren't enough. That you need to be patient and wait for the right time. That you have to accept things you hate in order to make progress bit by bit. You can't just run headlong into things and hope they turn out okay. That's how you get people killed."

"You standing by and listening to orders is what nearly go me killed."

He clenched his fists, his face twisting in pain and guilt and when he met my eyes his expression was raw. "You're right. It did. You're right."

"Maybe some idealism isn't the worst thing in the world." I crossed my arms protectively over my chest.

"Or maybe being around me is the worst thing for you, Apidae," he said, looking me over as if he was seeing me for the last time and he wanted to remember the sight. "I'm sorry. I'm sorry for everything and for dragging you into this. If I'd left you alone, none of this would have happened. I'll get you back to Ivo and he can take you somewhere safe – somewhere far from here and far from the revolution."

"You don't get to make decisions for me." I felt my jaw trembling. I'd gone through all of this and he thought I should just walk away now because … what? I hadn't been subtle enough in a meeting? I had shown too much emotion when seeing people tortured?

I shook my head in disbelief.

"Come on," he said gently, but he wouldn't meet my eyes now. He turned on his heel, stalking down the alley as he jammed one of his Forbidding-taken toothpicks in his teeth. He didn't even turn to see if I was following him.

I walked behind him, stinging with embarrassment and an undercurrent of rage. But I wasn't giving up. And I really did think that I could make a difference. No one else had seen that general. If I concentrated hard on the memory of him in the tower, I was sure I could find enough details in the landscape to find the tower. Once you were close, you'd be sure to see it. And it had to be in Far Stones or the snake people wouldn't have had it as part of their collective knowledge or history or whatever that awful stream of visions they'd given me was.

I would find him. And of course, he would want to fight with us. After all, he'd been left to rot in that tower by the Winged Empire and the snake people both. And then I'd show Osprey how wrong he was and how maybe my way wasn't so bad after all. It was certainly better than cowering and accepting everything the way he did.

I was so smug in my thoughts that I hardly noticed we'd reached the docks. We came out of the alley into a main street that led through the city wall, descending into broad stone steps that led to the port where the river met the ocean. Seabirds screamed through the air and white-wood totems bore their images everywhere.

Osprey stalked through the growing crowds – so thick now that if I didn't stay directly behind him I lost sight of him almost immediately – like a predator among prey. They parted for him, hitching their wide-legged trousers up nervously. One woman gave him a hopeful, assessing look, her eyes drifting over his broad shoulders and angled face, but when he ignored her, she simply shrugged and went back to work.

He caught more eyes than hers with the way his dark skin gleamed under the light of the seaside sun and the way he moved with purpose, his dark coat a single stain in a sea of whites and lighter sea-going colors. But he ignored everyone, his icy eyes fixed only on our destination.

The docks were already busy, men and women worked hauling canvas-wrapped bundles from ship boats or carting wheelbarrows of fish from boats already returning with their morning catch. Out at anchor a half-dozen larger ships bobbed, their small craft coming and going like water striders on a still pond. The cacophony of rattling wheels, cries of fishmongers, curses of people nearly tripped over, ship gongs and whistles nearly disoriented me until something flashed into the sky over everything – a large golden eagle flaring as it spun in the sky.

That's where Wing Ivo would be.

I grabbed Osprey's sleeve to point it out, but he gently removed my hand without looking in my direction.

"We'll be there in a moment and then you'll be free to leave with Ivo. This is for the best."

Irritated, I clenched my jaw and tried to appear to know what I was doing.

The docks seemed to be marked out. The white wood totems along them – while mostly of seabirds – were painted under the birds in patterns of color. One with yellow and white rings was filled with men in loose trousers and vests of the same color, working furiously to unload a pair of fishing vessels. Another totem featuring a kingfisher was painted with blue diamonds under the bird and the longshoremen there had blue diamonds embroidered on the backs of their vests and more blue diamonds on the small sleek white boats they used to bring passengers to and from the ships.

I was so proud of myself for figuring out how it worked that I nearly walked right into Osprey's back.

He had pulled up short right in front of Wing Ivo. Ivo was red-faced and arguing with a smaller woman. My jaw fell open as I realized it was Wing Xectare. She had survived! Her soft blonde hair was singed around the edges and a nasty burn marred one cheek, but her eyes glittered as she shook a finger at him.

"She was Essana's apprentice and Essana died. So, I will take the responsibility."

"It's the heart that makes the Wing and if you want to find a man with the biggest, savagest, most awe-inspiring heart, then that is me!" Wing Ivo was saying. "Will I take a second apprentice? You can bet I will! I'll take all the apprentices. And I'll train them properly. No more of this strict discipline and beating. Oh no, that's not how you raise a bird. How do you raise a bird, Xectare? You let her fly! She's got to fly! It's why she has Wings."

"Isn't it enough that you have the bee girl, Wing Ivo?" Xectare asked coolly. "I see she's arrived, and I see no bird in sight, which suggests that you haven't cured her of that stupidity. And if you have one poorly trained apprentice, it hardly proves that you can handle another apprentice."

Zayana stood halfway between them, making the sign of the bird as if she could ward herself from their argument. Behind her, a battered Counsellor Butiez whispered to the crown prince. He was surrounded by six stone-faced Claws, sitting in a folding chair someone had found him and leaning with his hands in his face, swaying side to side as if he could barely sit at all. Someone had given him a dark cloak with a deep hood, disguising his face, but I knew it was him. My bees buzzed in his torso. Beside me, Osprey stumbled slightly. Another wave from his bond with the prince.

What were they waiting for?

And then I heard the blare of a conch shell and the jingle of harnesses and cries from the crowd as they scrambled out of the way. I craned my neck to see what was happening and caught a glimpse of the Swan Banner flapping over the heads of a troop of Swan Claws riding carabaos down to the docks.

He must have been waiting for a proper escort.

I swallowed.

Whatever happened now, wouldn't be good for me. They would bring him to a healer and he wouldn't need my bees anymore – and that would be it. Osprey would kill me and any hope I had of saving my family and buying peace for our country would be over.

I glanced at Osprey. His eyes were shut tightly, his fists in tight balls. Maybe he was realizing the same thing I was. Or maybe the pain was finally too much for him, too.

My palms were getting sweaty as I tried to think of what to do next, my bees buzzing louder and louder as the tromp of the carabao hoofs on the boardwalk filled the air.

I needed a plan. I needed to get away right now. But everyone was right here and if I fled, I'd have to pass those carabaos.

"Fine!" Xectare spat. "You want to train a songbird with no potential and a girl with aberrations? Please yourself. I'm here to serve Le Majest as you should be."

"Indeed." Juste Montpetit's quiet word sliced through the noise like a knife even though they were muffled by the cloak. "You all serve at my leisure. You, Wing Ivo, have served as required. Take your new apprentice and go. No, not the bee girl. I will be holding on to her as my property."

"I'm her Guide, Le Majest, and I have ultimate say over her training." Wing Ivo didn't lack courage.

Juste Montpetit raised his head. His face was practically green it was so pale. Sweat ran in rivers down the sides of his face and he breathed slowly as if every breath was a struggle. In the hood of his cloak, just as disguised as he was, I saw the faintest hint of a glowing snake head. Its tongue flickered out as if tasting my nerves. I thought it might like the flavor. My hands began to shake, and I couldn't tear my eyes away from him.

"That's true in every circumstance except in that of property. I own this Hatchling as my personal property."

He raised a single eyebrow and Ivo swallowed his words, making the sign of the bird instead and grabbing Zayana's arm to disappear into the crowd. I caught her panicked eye as she left, and we exchanged a momentary look of sympathy. She didn't want to go with the wild Wing – that was obvious – and I did not want to remain here. I'd trade places with her in a heartbeat

– well, maybe not. It would be cruel to put anyone in the place I was in now.

"Get me a healer, Osprey. The best you can find. And bring her to me. I will be claiming the House of Sunsets. Fly with your bird if you must. That's an order."

"And the girl?" Osprey asked, gripping my arm.

"Leave her with me."

A bubble of dread welled up in me as Osprey made the sign of the bird and then his osprey appeared and he leapt onto its back, speeding over the heads of the crowd and leaving me with my worst enemy and all his fury.

CHAPTER EIGHTEEN

The boardwalk shivered under the hooves of the carabaos as they pulled up in front of Juste Montpetit. The Swan Claw on the lead animal leapt from the saddle, bowing low and making the sign of the bird. Around us, gasps filled the crowd as they scrambled to follow his example.

"Le Majest!"

Juste Montpetit threw off the hood of his cloak, tilting his chin high as if to give the sky a glimpse of his beautiful face. The strain of pretending to be healthy made his expression tight and pained.

Stillness filled the docks as everyone froze mid-action or dropped to their knees. I could almost hear my racing heart.

"It is our great honor to serve, Le Majest," the captain of the Swan Claws said, kneeling down on his fine trousers, his impeccable blue jacket trimmed with white swan feathers. The cord wrapped around his forehead matched the jacket perfectly. "All is being prepared for you in the House of Sunset."

Juste Montpetit flicked a finger as the guard stood, offering his carabao with a gesture. At Juste's sneer, they brought forward a carabao with an enclosed chair strapped to its back. Likely, they thought him an arrogant prince. I knew he didn't have the strength to ride. He was fighting to stand straight and I could feel the pull on my strength as my bees buzzed doubly hard to keep him upright. The cloak hid them from view, but their sound was loud enough that people in the crowd looked nervously around them as if wondering whether they'd disturbed a wasp nest.

The snake – Sephilis – was hidden again. I wondered if it was possible to wring his neck. Zayana's bird had been damaged. If you could damage a spirit bird, could you kill a spirit snake?

"Better," the crown prince proclaimed as they brought him the enclosed chair. The guard's expression showed pure relief.

I started to edge away slowly. In all this confusion, they'd forget about me. This was my chance to escape. Even Osprey was gone.

I ducked behind a totem pole, controlling my breathing, carefully making myself small.

A hand grabbed my sleeve and pulled me out from behind the pole and Counsellor Butiez whispered in my ear, his breath heavy with garlic.

"I've been two days in this city already and do you know what I've heard? Someone pulled our Claws out of Far Reach. Someone who wrote a missive in my hand and put it on one of my birds. Any ideas who that might be?"

"It's a mystery," I choked out.

"I'm given to understand that you are necessary as long as those bees hold my lord together. But Osprey is already on his way to find a healer. And I think that girls who write lies should lose their hands. Don't you?"

"I think that Counsellors who whisper poison should lose their tongues."

My mouth was so dry that I barely got the words out, but I refused to give in to him and let him see that he scared me – that his whole awful empire scared me. I needed a way out. And I needed it now.

I clenched my jaw, feeling for my bees. They buzzed in response. They were ready.

So was I.

"Take her!" I heard Butiez telling someone, but my vision vanished as my mind filled with buzzing and I saw Ixtep now on the top of a hill, surrounded by hundreds of his masked people. He was looking down at something below him.

I was looking through my bee's eyes, I realized. That was why the view was so jittery and hard to see. I fought nausea, straining to see through the eyes of something that flew in mad bursts and arcs. Wait. The city they were looking down on looked very familiar. It had spires. And bronze birds on the spires … he was watching Karkatua!

My vision cleared and I leaned over, vomiting down the side of the carabao I'd been hoisted onto. The soldier holding me cursed.

"I just polished this tack!"

Cobbles raced under me as we rode the carabao into the city.

But the visions weren't over. My eyes darkened again, and I saw Ixtap raise his arm and then lower it quickly in a chopping motion. There was a roar. Bodies moving.

And I was vomiting again. Someone cuffed me in the back of the head.

"Would you stop it, you lunatic?"

If only I had the kind of control to do just that. Stomach clenching, I drew my bees to me. There was a scream from the front of the carabao line where Juste's enclosed chair was positioned. We were inside the city walls, I realized. And we were about to be attacked by his snake buddies.

I barely had time to suck in a deep breath when the conch shells began to blare, and bells began to ring.

"Get the crown prince to safety!" the Swan Claw Captain shouted and then the carabaos were running, screams echoing all around as the crowd tried to part for them in the narrow city street.

The soldier behind me was white-faced, his eyes on the nearest city wall.

This was my chance.

I took it.

I pulled my bees to me, whispering to them, "Please, distract them, distract them."

I felt a buzz of agreement and then we were surrounded by the cloud of my bees as I wrenched myself from the grip of the screaming Claw who had been holding me only a moment before. My feet hit the cobblestones with a jarring crash, but I didn't wait to assess injuries, I just ran.

I darted into the nearest alley, not stopping to look behind me, pushing all my speed into my flight. This was my one chance to get away while they were all distracted. And I could do it now. My family was out of harm's way. Osprey was distracted. Le Majest's city was under attack. What could they possibly do?

A length of cloth was strung over a clothesline in the alley. A dropcloth for a worker, perhaps, or a bedsheet. It was a dark gray.

I snatched it from the line, swathed it around me like a cloak, and kept running. I needed to disguise my fine coat and tight breeches. They'd look for those. If they looked at all.

The horns blared again from the walls. The city was under attack. Would they even have time to look for me?

I shot out of the alley and into a street, hurrying past a frantic street vendor who was trying to pull all his fruit back inside his cart. Screams and shouted orders filled the streets. Desperate eyes darted over mine as families tried to gather frightened children and shops tried to close up to protect their merchandise.

Had this city seen an attack like this before? Possibly. Back when the General with two ravens was here. But that was a long time ago. I darted into another alley, trying to make my way toward the wall. I needed to get out of the city, or I'd be trapped here when they shut the gates. If I was trapped here, then I'd never get away.

I scrambled through the crowds of people, filling even the alleys now as they hurried to shelter in their homes or to man the walls. I'd been close to the walls already. I could see them over the roofs of the houses nearby, but getting through the crowds and the maze of streets was tougher than I would have guessed. Whoever built this city hadn't thought that gaps between buildings were necessary.

I was almost there. If I could just find my way out of this maze. Someone bumped into me, screaming curses as her basket of spring greens hit the ground and scattered in the mud. A rough man – a tavern bouncer, perhaps – shoved me out of his way and I stumbled against a building, bruising my side. At least there were no Claws here. They had other problems to deal with.

A pair of chickens flew the coop, flying into my face. I batted them away and stumbled past, slipping in something I didn't want to identify and running headlong into a carabao team. The driver flicked his whip and pain seared across my cheek. I reached up and felt blood.

"Clear the street!" he yelled as I stumbled back.

"Find us the right path," I whispered to my bees and I felt them hum in harmony with me. They wanted that, too. The best path, the right path, the path for the swarm.

They sped out from me like tiny arrows and I sighed in relief at the feeling of them flying. I hadn't realized how tense I'd felt when they were in Montpetit's belly – but it was like knots were being released in my muscles. I could move again.

I followed the bee nearest me and then another joined it and they shifted their direction and still I followed through the chaos of the shrieking crowd.

We stumbled around a corner and there it was. The gate.

I sped from the alley and out into the wide avenue leading to the city gate. The Claws there were shouting at the crowd as they hurried in through the gates.

"Make way! The gates must be closed!"

But there were too many people flooding through for the heavy gates to close easily. They moved an inch at a time as the Claws fought against the river of people. I could still make it out of Karkatua if I hurried.

I fought against the stream of wild-eyed people, ignoring curses and flying elbows as I pushed my way against the tide of their bodies. Their eyes were wide like panicked horses caught in a trap. I swallowed down my own fear. The last thing I wanted was to be a panicked farm animal. I needed to be brave and sure.

Blackness flashed across my vision and I stumbled at a momentary vision of Wing Ivo scrambling with Zayana to find a place on the walls.

"Not helpful!" I muttered, forcing my feet forward even as my vision was still obscured.

I managed another step and then a second wave of blackness hit me. My bee had found Osprey, wild-eyed, flying an older woman with a basket of vials over the frantic crowd. He was cursing such a stream of vile threats that I thought he must be talking to me. He was looking directly at my bee.

Come on, Aella!

My vision flickered again and now I was seeing Brielle – the Claw I'd just met this morning. She was standing beside a high-ranking Claw on the wall.

"… too fast," he was saying. "We can't organize quickly enough for this. They're going to roll over us like a wave. Who are these people?"

"We can send messengers," Brielle suggested.

He scoffed. "Unless you know someone who can see what's happening everywhere in Karkatua at once and report it to me, we can't respond fast enough. Take a contingent to the Crown Prince. Get him on a ship immediately. All troops are ordered to abandon the city."

My vision returned, but I froze, staring at the city gate as it slowly closed. If I left through that gate, I'd be abandoning this entire city to its fate, just like that Claw commander. We had people in this city coordinating the rebellion.

Beside me, a child wailed as his mother scooped him up, running with tears streaming down her face.

And what would happen to innocent children like him? I'd seen the thirst for blood and revenge in the hearts of the snakes. They'd slaughter these innocents as easily as Juste Montpetit would abandon them.

I drew in a long breath. There would be no running for me today. I knew what I had to do.

It was all I could do to turn away from my chance of escape, to watch as the way out of the city slowly closed, locking me inside. But I'd made my choice. If you lost your fight, you lost yourself.

"Scatter," I whispered to my bees. "I need to see everything in this city – every vantage from the wall, every gate, every leader who braces the walls for battle. And one of you needs to find Wing Ivo. And another should stay near the prince."

They were already scattering as I finished breathing my request. We were the swarm. We would defend our hive.

I turned on my heel away from the gates and my hopes of escape.

CHAPTER NINETEEN

I hurried through the crowds of distressed people. Most of the civilians were streaming into the city, while groups of Claws ran outward toward the walls. Like two rivers running in opposite directions, side by side, they poured through the avenues and streets, sweeping up anyone in their paths.

I had a moment of dizziness as another flash of vision seared across my mind – Ixtap raced across the land, his snake rising before him as he reached the walls.

That's where I needed to be if I wanted to help defend Karkatua. On the walls.

I angled toward them, falling in line behind a group of Claws in short bright-blue coats thick with white stitching. We rounded a corner toward a wide staircase leading up to the walls. The men in front of me ran up the staircase, but I paused. Now what? I'd run into this without knowing what to do next. If only my bees could tell me where Ivo was, or someone else who might know what to do.

A Claw cleared half the stairs in a leap, landing beside me as she regained her balance.

Brielle! I reached out and grabbed her.

"Hands off!" she bellowed.

"Claw Brielle!" I objected, holding on tightly to her.

"I have orders to join the crown prince," she said grimly without turning. I clung to her jacket, pulled along by her momentum. "Civilians are barred from the wall. Leave immediately."

"Stop!"

She turned for just long enough to recognize me, shaking her head as soon as she did.

"I'm not your nursemaid. Go find Osprey. He'll take you in hand."

"I can help!" I said, certainty I didn't have filling my voice.

Brielle looked both ways before grabbing my collar and hauling me into an alley, shoving me against a worn plaster wall.

"Now isn't time for revolutions or militia, girl. The city is under attack. I have Claw business."

I nodded. "You have to get the crown prince onto a ship." Her jaw dropped but I plowed on. "My bees can scatter all across the city and report to me. Clearly, that's a needed skill right now."

She nodded once, curtly.
"There's a small gatehouse on top of the wall where the seagull flag flies. Inside are those who will lead the defense. Offer this talent to them. If anyone tries to bar you from the wall, give them my name and for sky's sake, girl, don't embarrass me."

She was gone before I could reply, arrowing through the crowds toward the docks.

I gritted my teeth and ran back toward the stairs, elbowing my way through groups of Claws waiting for orders at the base of the stairs. As I ran, I snatched a polearm from a stash of supplies.

"Stop!" one of the Claws stationed next to the stack called after me. "Those are for Claws only! The citizenry is not to be armed!"

Even under attack, they clung to their ridiculous new ideals.

I barely paused. "I'm under orders from Claw Brielle."

He opened his mouth, but I ignored him, hurtling up the steps and onto the wall. At the crest of the steps, I wavered, falling forward to one knee and losing my polearm.

A vision flashed before my eyes. The crown prince screaming, hands clenched to where the honeycomb in his belly held him together as a middle-aged woman spoke frantically beside him. Osprey held the crowd back, stumbling and shaking his head as the Claws ringing the prince stood in a white-faced ring around them.

Osprey pulled his toothpick from his lips, looked directly at my bee, and cursed as he fell to one knee.

"Stay there," I whispered to the bee. "Stay with him."

My vision swam back and I pulled myself to my feet, tottering slightly as I regained my place on the last step and leaned on the wicked-tipped polearm to steady me as I worked my way across the wall to the gatehouse. The wall was nearly as wide as an alley, but already it bristled with soldiers readying their defenses.

"You there!" One of them called to me. "Get off the wall!"

I sped up, hoping to hurry past before they could stop me, but another man leaned out from the wall, his arm reaching out to grab me. I blinked when I realized it was Ames, still wearing his blacksmith apron, a blue armband around his arm.

"Citizen militia," he said warily. "By order, all citizens without the armband must remove themselves from the wall."

"Then you'd better get me an armband," I said, setting my jaw determinedly. "I can see everything happening in the city and I need to get to the guardhouse."

He opened his mouth as a green glow washed over him. Before he could speak, I grabbed his apron, trying to pull him with me as I threw myself to the ground.

"Get down!" I said but pulling him was like trying to pull a rock five times my weight. He didn't budge.

Above me, something screamed – high-pitched and horrifying. The buzzing in my head intensified. I shrank against the earth as the snake head plunged from the sky before us, wrapping itself around the man beside Ames with a mighty gulp.

My heart pounded in my chest as I scrambled to my feet again and jabbed at the snake with my stolen polearm. This must be the point of attack. But no. My vision flickered and I was somewhere else along the wall. Screams filled the air as a snake manifestation rippled between the defenders. Flickered again and there was one coming in from under the gate. Flickered again and there was one rising to fight us from out of the sea.

I fell to my knees, clutching my head.

The buzzing was so loud, I could hardly think. I'd dropped the polearm. Someone was pulling me. But I wasn't seeing with my own eyes, I was seeing with the eyes of the swarm.

Flash.

Osprey snarling at me – no, at my bee! – as the healer yelled that the prince was losing consciousness.

Flash.

Another snake over the wall like a grappling rope – but a grappling rope that could fight. It snatched a defender from her post, swallowing her into his semi-transparent magic body. Unlike a real snake, there was no bulge where she had once been. She was simply there one moment in her bright blue jacket, screaming defiance, and then gone the next.

Flash and I saw Wing Ivo thundering through the crowds, his bird sweeping up to the wall in a flash of gold. Beside him, a pale-faced Zayana had her hands stretched wide for her bird to sail ahead of them.

Flash.

I fought the visions. I needed to see what was happening to me in my actual body before I was eaten by a spirit snake. My heart was pounding so hard I could hardly catch my breath.

My vision cleared for just long enough to see I was being dragged into the gatehouse by Ames.

"This is no place for civilians!" a Claw roared. "Get out!"

"The girl claims she can see all over the city!" Ames said. "She can tell us where the attacks are!"

"And my aged mother claims she can see the face of the girl you will marry in a tub of dishes. Out!"

We were shoved out and my vision clouded again. There were too many snakes crawling up the wall where the red flags were. "How do I tell one place from another?"

Ames grunted. "They're marked by the scarves. Flags that are posted. Look for the ones with the seagull totem and a color. Those tell you whether it is north, south, east, or west."

My vision had already flashed back to Ixtap, his face full of triumph as he rode on the back of a snake as broad as a horse. I shuddered.

"Red," I gasped. "They are sending more snakes to red."

"What are these snakes?" Ames asked. "A nightmare come alive?"

"Manifestations," I gasped.

I felt his hand leave me as I sank into the next vision. In the background, I heard him fighting with the Claw to let him in again.

Flash. Fight on the wall. People falling, arms windmilling as they screamed.

Flash. A glimpse of my brother Oska's face. That couldn't be right.

Flash. Zayana's mouth wide open as Wing Ivo's eagle dove and snatched a snake out of the air seconds before its jaws closed around her. It struggled, writhing in the air as he gained height.

"Go!" Ivo screamed at her and she scrambled forward, fast and graceful as a dancer, weaving between fighters effortlessly. Her bird was showing its power in that.

Flash. Masked snake people pouring over the wall, running up the backs of the snake manifestations.

I needed a better way to see these visions than in flashes like this! This couldn't be how bees saw all the time … could it?

And then there were gentle hands on me.

"She doesn't look hurt."

"Zayana," I gasped. "Graceful as the most talented dancer."

I wasn't even making sense. My visions were flickering too fast as my bees grew frantic. I needed them to calm down.

Flash. A man fell from the wall, hands grasping for his friend above. His friend's face a gut-wrenching mask of loss. He twisted in terror as his fingers caught at nothing.

Flash. A woman clutching a child as a snake manifestation escaped the wall and chased her fleeing through the streets. Her breath was so loud in her throat that it sounded as if it would saw her in half.

My eyes popped open.

"Purple flags. They've breached the wall. Snakes in the streets."

"We need to tell the Claws," Ivo said, emerging from behind Zayana. His face was streaked with dirt and sweat and his breath came quickly from the fighting.

"Do you believe her?" Zayana asked. "How could she know that?"

I could hear Ames explaining the situation to Ivo. About the Claws throwing him out. About the militia ready but needing orders. He must know Ivo was a Single Wing.

I gasped as my vision filled with a snake creeping up the wall, ten others behind him. A snake ridden by Ixtap.

"Ixtap," I gasped. "With ten other snakes. They creep up a wall with blue flags."

Ames cursed, pushing up to look over the wall.

"Don't look, you fool!" Ivo hissed. "Zayana! Did you learn the language of the scarves in your training as an Imperial High'un?"

"Yes," Zayana whispered.

"Then come on." He grabbed my arm and pulled me up a ladder on the side of the gatehouse. I could barely find the rungs, but Zayana, coming up from behind me, doggedly put my feet into the right ones as I swayed, bucking under the constant shift of visions. My stomach was ill. My head wasn't made for heights and now we were on the roof of a guardhouse on the top of a wall over a gate. I swayed as we reached the top. A wall that went only to my knees rimmed the roof – just enough wall to remind a person where the edges were.

There were silk flags all over the ground and two frantic Claws were working the flags, raising and lowering them as someone called up orders through a hole in the floor. They were both young, their Claw jackets fresh and bright. One of them paused, staring at Ivo with round, terrified eyes.

"Stop!" Ivo roared. "I am Imperial Wing Ivo of House Golden Eagle and I am commandeering this flag post." He shoved Zayana to the flags. "Raise the flags as I give orders." He turned to his bird. "Defend this guardhouse with all power. None shall gain access. Go!"

"Now," he said, leaning in close to me. "Let's see what those bees can do."

CHAPTER TWENTY

It was like a nightmare that wouldn't end.

"He's over the edge of the wall, where the purple banners are, riding a snake," I gasped as the vision took me. Claws fell – screaming – horror filling their faces as the snake hurtled between them. Two Claws braced themselves on the wall as the spirit snake's body rippled over the summit. The leather bands holding their hair back lashed as they looked back and forth to either side of the wall. Their eyes met and with a grim nod to each other, they charged.

They had to know it was a doomed attempt. They had to know the snake could crush them like insects, and yet they rushed forward, courage filling their faces, swords held in both hands. The swords plunged into the snake and he trembled.

For a moment, it seemed their sacrifice was worth it, and then the snake bucked. Their swords were wrenched upward, but the Claws held on as they were flung into the air and then smashed down again. Teeth gritted, they readied themselves to be bucked again as they wrenched their swords back and forth in the body of the snake. My bee didn't see its head snaking back until the jaw opened and gulped down the Claws in a single bite.

I shuddered.

"How many are falling?" Ivo asked.

"The whole defense," I gasped, clutching my ringing head, eyes closed. "At least a hundred. Oh, sweet skies and winds! The other snake has wrapped around the tower."

A snake warrior dropped from the back of the snake, waving a spear above his head with an ululating cry that echoed across the defenses. Behind him, others rushed over the wall like black ants, their scale mail shimmering in the sun.

"Raise the flag for 'retreat to nearest point of strength' and the 'east' flag," Ivo called to Zayana. He grabbed my shoulder, keeping me with him for a moment. "What do you see now?"

I closed my eyes and a new bee flickered to life.

"Claw Brielle has reached Le Majest with a group of a hundred Claws to escort him to the ships."

She was bellowing orders in a voice so deep it made *me* want to snap to attention, her fingers darting in a language made of signs that saw her Claws spread out, surrounding Le Majest and clearing a path toward the port wall.

"Not that!" Ivo shook my shoulder. "What about the east wall?"

"I don't control what I see!" I gasped.

Ivo cursed. "Then see faster."

I saw faster.

"A family – they're fleeing down the street. Oh, please save them! Please! The child!" I felt tears streaking my face. It was too late. I closed my jaw with a snap, but though I couldn't help them, I couldn't stop seeing.

"Any landmarks?" Ivo barked.

I shook myself. "A fountain. Like a falcon."

"Raise the flag for 'Hold in Place.' And the gold flag." Ivo's orders were sharp and fast. In the background, I heard the sound of pulleys and ropes as Zayana and the two Claws hurried to raise flags. "Then raise the flag "Marshall" and the orange flag. That should send any reserves to that sector to fight the breach."

"We can't survive a breach like this!" one of the Claws muttered. "We've already lost the east wall. The city is open."

"If you can't speak hope then at least have the decency to speak the language of the wise – silence!" Irritation burred Ivo's voice. "More, Aella. Dive into the nightmare and bring us back pearls."

"The nearest flag station is questioning our orders," Zayana called. "They say they are overriding the orders of … House Frigatebird?"

"The Claw Captain in the guardhouse under us," Ivo said shortly as I rocked back and forth, seeing what I didn't want to see over and over again. My breath was coming too fast. I needed to concentrate to remember to breathe evenly. "Use the flags to tell them I am Wing Ivo of House Golden Eagle and I am taking over command of these defenses."

Above us, his golden eagle screamed and then dove again. How did he manage to invoke it while doing all of this? I needed more control. I needed my bees to hear me rather than forcing me to dance to their hum.

I tried to focus on all of them at once so I could try to send them that idea. My eyes crossed like I was trying to pick out someone wrapped in drabs lying under the leaves. And then, with a painful twist, my eyes seemed to change how they were seeing. I crossed into some new mental sense – and I saw it all at once.

The view snapped away from me almost as soon as I had it. I reeled, gasping. "They're trying to distract us on the east wall so we won't see that they've slipped in around the docks. They have snakes swimming through the water toward the ships. It's a trap," I gasped.

"Mmm," Wing Ivo said, his face screwing up in concentration.

"Osprey is taking Le Majest to a ship for safety," I whispered.

"See more," he ordered, standing to give orders.

I leaned my weary head against the wall, crossed my mental eyes, and let myself drift in the strange world where I saw everything else. With it came a strange sense of detachment as if nothing really was real.

"The Claws sent to the fountain square are all dead. There are more snakes there. They're bursting through the walls of houses, going from house to house and killing everything in their paths. No, not that … please." I could see the carnage, the death. I tried pinching my eyes shut, but it kept coming.

"What else girl? What else?"

"There are children," I gasped.

"Focus! Deal with the horror after. Right now, we need your eyes. See for us!"

I shook myself and forced myself to really see. "It's a distraction from what they really want. I see a group of the masked ones on foot, led by Ixtap. They follow his snake through the streets, hunting. I don't know what they hunt for. They are getting close to the center of the city. They've met little resistance. All the Claws are at the walls and the citizens are unarmed. The north wall is overrun. The east wall has fallen. Snakes everywhere, hanging over the wall. Everywhere. We need to fight them back before any Claws can retake the wall."

I felt like I'd only been talking for seconds, but when my vision cleared again, Ivo and Zayana looked worn, the Claws beside them leaned against the wall for support. I'd been feeding them a steady stream of information. I swayed, clutching the wall as nausea rolled over me.

"We need to give her a rest, Wing Ivo, or she will overdo it and collapse," Zayana warned.

"If she falls, we all fall, apprentice," Ivo said wearily. He was at the edge of the short wall and based on his arm gestures, he was directing his eagle. "Back in, girl. See for us."

"They're coming for our tower here," I gasped. "They're gathering at the base."

Wing Ivo looked over the edge and cursed.

"We can't stay here. The Claws are pulling back from the wall and abandoning the post below."

"Why would they do that?" Zayana asked.

"House Frigatebird must be abandoning the walls," one of the Claws helping us said. "Our contingency is to flee to the ships."

"And the population of the city?" Zayana asked in horror.

The Claw shrugged. "We've been told the security of Le Majest is our top priority. Anything else is not our concern. If the city can't be held, we'll take him to safety."

"This is insane!"

"Gather the flags," Ivo ordered. "You're staying with us."

"It's too late," I gasped. The snakes below were climbing the wall, warriors flinging themselves onto the backs of the spirit snakes and holding on for dear life. We had minutes at most to abandon the tower top.

Harpy dove from above shrieking and Ivo grabbed my arm, pushing me toward the ladder.

"Climb down. You two watch the Hatchling!"

I tried to climb down, tried to block out the visions I was seeing, but I slipped, falling the last three steps to the top of the wall. I heard Zayana's worried cries, but my mind was filled again with visions.

I saw people in plain clothes, armed, forming up across the city, leaping out in small knots for a surprise attack here, or to take back a square there. If we could just get word to them, they could coordinate.

"Can the militia read the flags?" I asked, gasping as Zayana pulled me to my feet.

"We'll need somewhere high up. An upper floor of a building or somewhere similar," Wing Ivo said as he shoved me toward the stairs leading down from the wall. "But yes, they can read them."

"They're forming up. But there aren't enough in any one place to make a difference. They need to work together."

"Then we need somewhere high." He hurried me down the steps, giving curt orders to the Claws. "Give Hatchling Zayana all the flags. No, she can carry them, it isn't far. Draw on your bird, girl. Take from him the lightness of flying things and the speed of a bird on the wing. No, no! Not that way. Can't you see that the Claws are going that way? We need somewhere unexpected."

Twice he grabbed me by the collar and pulled me along when

the visions overwhelmed me. We were on the streets by the time we broke free of the retreating Claws and were in the city, hurrying between the homes and businesses as Ivo stared up at their upper levels.

"Somewhere high," he muttered. "Somewhere easy to see."

We were close to where Osprey and I had entered the city mere hours ago.

"The tailor," I gasped. "There is a bridge between the rooftops."

He nodded as I pointed vaguely toward it.

Another vision rocked me, making me stumble and my sight go dark.

Ixtap plunged through the city like a knife, his snake beside him, lashing out in every direction as citizens fled screaming. It came to the place where the men were rotting in their stocks and the snake reared up, crashing toward the poor victims of the Empire with its jaws wide. I gritted my teeth against their screams.

When I blinked my eyes open Ivo had me over his shoulder as he climbed the steps up to the rickety walkway.

"Perfect choice," he muttered. And then, louder, he said, "The brown flag, Zayana. The moment you get there, start waving it!"

My vision darkened and now all I saw was flames as the east gate was lit. Beside my bee, men with grim faces and the clothing of workers gathered together. One wore a floury apron, streaks of flour on his face. He brandished a huge poker from his bakery ovens, no doubt. Another wore the leathers of a carter, a carabao horn in each hand. There was a boy Alect's age holding a cast iron frying pan in trembling hands. It dripped grease as if it had been pulled hot off the fire. They'd had to make do with what they could find. But anything could be a weapon when need and desperation made it so.

"Do we have a chance, Bruit?" the baker asked and an older man missing one of his eyes drew a sword from his belt. The scabbard was worked with woodpeckers. He must have hidden it away somehow.

"We'll keep tapping until they fall. That's the motto of House Woodpecker," the old man said with a frown. "Hold your nerve boys. Wait for my sign."

"The flag!" the boy cried. "It's brown."

"That's for militia. Now's our time," the old man said. "And if any of you lives until tomorrow, Pendre here will cook them eggs and wing toast, won't you boy."

The boy nodded, but he couldn't seem to stop trembling.

"Don't worry boy. Just watch our backs," the old man said, softening. "Go, Baker!"

And then they were charging toward the enemy, weapons raised, a battle cry in their throat.

"War and Wings!"

I blinked back to where we were, balanced on the narrow catwalk.

"The militia is fighting," I gasped.

"Signal a counter-attack from the Wings," Ivo ordered. "They'll need back up."

My vision blurred and then I saw the Healer struggling over Le Majest. He lay on the cobbles, eyes rolled back in his head. Osprey kneeled beside him, head bowed. He was struggling along with the prince. They'd made it almost to the docks.

Behind them, one of the ships went down at anchor, a snake wrapping around it and crushing it to splinters. Os plunged through the air to tear another snake to pieces before it could crush a second ship.

I babbled what I was seeing to Ivo and he relayed orders to Zayana and the Wings.

I saw and saw and saw until I was so tired my eyes would barely stay open.

The tide was turning. We'd taken back the wall. We'd closed the breach in the gate. We'd stopped the snakes before they could crush more than two ships.

Ixtap ravaged through the city, hunting for something. But why? What reason would he have to attack now with only part of his forces? I could tell this wasn't all of them. I'd seen many more at the Cobra Temple. Besides, he was allied with Le Majest. They had spent days together. Was all that only a ruse?

But no.

As his party swept into the square where the ring of Claws stood around their fallen prince, he took one look at them, at the massive purplish-white Osprey hovered over them, and he quickly turned, speeding in the other direction.

My vision shifted and I was back with the militia, watching as the Baker fell to a spear through the throat. The old man was on his knees, still hacking with his woodpecker sword. Behind him, the boy stepped forward, tears streaking his face as he brought the frying pan down on the head of one of the snake warriors and snatched the spear from his hands.

I blinked and for a moment I thought I was looking with

my bees, but no, these were my real eyes. Below the catwalk we were on, Ixtap and his snake stood quietly looking up at me. His mouth slowly curled upward at the corners.

"They're right below us." I hardly recognized my own voice, it was so raw.

Zayana gasped.

"The door!" Ivo ordered and the Claws hurried to Osprey's round door, jiggling the handle.

"Key," I gasped as the delicate stairway began to shake with weight. The snake was slithering upward. "In my pocket."

Zayana's hand dipped into my jacket pocket and then they were fumbling with the lock.

My vision flickered and then I was looking up at myself from Ixtap's shoulder. I was watching as the Claws burst into the round door. Watching as they dragged my senseless form behind them.

Ixtap clicked his tongue. As if it was some kind of a signal, the snake began to draw back.

"Drawing back," I said through thick lips as the door slammed behind us, the lock clicking back into place. I was past tired. Past thirsty.

"Easy," Zayana's voice was comforting as she helped me to the pallet in the corner. I collapsed heavily into it. It smelled of Osprey and just like that, my vision was back to him.

In my mind's eye, I saw Osprey clamber to his feet in shock. The color was back in his cheeks. His movements were strong. Before him, Le Majest rose to his feet in front of the dock gates. His shirt was off and his too-pale skin reflected the brightness of the sun. My honeycomb was still in his belly, but he looked strong now, his face pink and flushed. He leaned on the smiling healer and began to speak, a pleasant smile on his face.

A look of horror flooded Osprey's face.

"Le Majest is healed," I muttered.

My vision flickered. The last snake slithered from the north wall.

I reported it dutifully, but though my vision continued to take everything in, my mind was haunted by that look in Osprey's eyes.

I watched the boy with the skillet standing tall over his friends as the last snake retreated before him. He kneeled to touch the old man, but his friend's eyes were glazed with death. The boy's shoulder's slumped.

I began to shake on the pallet. I couldn't keep my eyes open anymore.

"Don't fade yet, Bees!" Wing Ivo called to me. "It's almost done!"

My vision flickered again and I watched a Claw snatch a child from the street moments before a spirit snake slithered by at full speed. The Claw dashed into an open doorway, depositing the sobbing child into the arms of his mother. They fell to the floor together in cries of relief.

And we really *were* done.

My bees watched Ixtap as he and his men fled through the breach in the wall, my solitary bee fleeing with them.

And every vision was one of relief and rescue, of friends pulling friends out from the rubble of fires tamed and tears of joy.

But why attack in the first place if they weren't willing to see it through? We hadn't beaten them back. Our losses far outweighed theirs. It was as if they'd done their job and then left. But what, exactly, had that job been?

Exhaustion rolled over me like a cloud over the sun and with it came the darkness of unconsciousness.

CHAPTER TWENTY-ONE

I woke to gentle hands lifting me – which seemed at odds to the almost panicked tone in Wing Ivo's voice.

"It doesn't make any sense. She won that for us. She saw everything, Osprey. Those bees – they're better than you could imagine on a battlefield! Not a secret maneuver, not an enemy action, not so much as a blink that we missed, and it was all her manifestations. And – of course, Zayana – and her quick hands on the ropes. You're a master with those scarves girl! A real master, caster, raster of a High'un and I'll take you into the breach and back with me on any day of the Forbidding-taken week!"

I moaned as I struggled for consciousness.

"She ran, Ivo." Osprey's voice was nearly a whisper.

"*To* battle, Osprey. Not away from it. Without her, we would have lost the city. She was glorious!"

"She took her bees. She left Le Majest to die."

"Is he dead?" Ivo sounded mulish. "No? Then I'm guessing she didn't leave him to die. I'm guessing she left him with you – who, by the way, would have been a lot of use in a battle against massive spirit snakes rather than tied to a princeling like a pretty sash. She went off to do the real work of defending innocents and saving this city. She's exactly what we hoped for, Osprey! Exactly what was prophesied. A turning point. And a turning point with *heart.* A turning point with *power.* Those bees are going to change everything for us. The possibilities have me tingling. Tingling."

I could feel my bees returning to me a little at a time. I was gaining strength with every one that returned to my core. My eyes fluttered open.

Ivo smiled down at me. "Nice work, bees. You did good. Keep up the meditation and who knows how high you'll buzz."

I tried to speak but all that came out was a groan.

"Leave her here and I'll tend her," Ivo said, still grinning proudly like a mother with a new baby.

"It's like you aren't listening to me, Ivo," Osprey said through gritted teeth. "I'm here for her on the order of Le Majest."

"Don't tell me the boy prince has come to his senses and is ready to thank her properly," he still sounded triumphant, but my heart was sinking. The tension in Osprey's shoulders, the way his face was outlined with stress – this wasn't good. This wasn't thanks at all. Wait. Was I in his arms?

I struggled to try to get my feet under me, but I barely shifted in his grasp. I'd used every shred of energy in the battle.

Osprey growled low in his throat. "If she lives through the night, we'll both be lucky. Le Majest is slathering for blood. You should have had better sense than this *Guide.*"

The blood drained from Ivo's face and he reached for me, but he was too late. Osprey turned so quickly that nausea washed over me and then he stepped, and the familiar weightlessness washed over me. The feeling of being borne up into the sky over updrafts and through swirls of breeze was almost becoming usual. I tried to think only of that and not of how I could barely lift my eyelids or of what new horror awaited me at our destination.

"When they tied every thread of my being to the lives of innocents and told me to dance, I thought that was the only hell I'd have to suffer through until my eventual death, but you bring me to greater depths of agony," Osprey was saying as he carried me. I didn't know if he knew I could hear. He seemed almost to be speaking to himself. "The monks of the Golden Spire say that through suffering we are redeemed. If that is true, then I have been redeemed from every vein of evil running through my heart, but I don't believe it's true. What is suffering when it has no point? What is agony if it has no end?"

"There's a point," I whispered.

He startled. He must really have thought I was not able to listen.

"I don't know if I believe that anymore." He sounded so lost. "I'd hoped to change things – to help someone else bring in a new brighter future, even if I could never be a part of it, even if I would have to watch from the sidelines wearing the face and hands of a traitor, even if my death would eventually water the seeds of a new nation. But you wear my hopes to tatters, you grind me down and hollow my bones."

"Thank you for the key to your home." I could afford courtesy at the very least.

He grunted. "It's not the only key you've given me."

I was having trouble focusing. I tried to pull on my bees, searching for the energy to speak.

"I know why you're saying all of this," I said grimly. My belly felt like water was sloshing in it as I spoke my worst fears. "You're about to torture me for him, aren't you? Just like you did to my father. And you want me to believe that your coming actions are my fault and not yours. You want to blame them on someone else because doing that will make it easier for you to live with yourself when you're done."

"No." His word was like a plea.

"Don't lie to me," I said weakly. My whole body felt like someone had stuck a tap into it and left it running until it was dry. The magic I'd used for my bees had sucked me dry. None of them buzzed around me now. I couldn't even hear their hum. "You're trapped. You're owned. And you are flailing, trying to think of a way out of it one moment and then just accepting it the next. You're too terrified of the consequences of outright rebellion but you still have too much hope to give up. So, you'll torture me for your master and you'll hate yourself for every minute of it."

"What else can I do?" he asked weakly. "There is no way out. I'm trapped until I die. I just … I'd hoped for a minute … I don't know why I was such a fool as to hope." He snorted grimly. "There's never a point in hoping. We're all as entrapped as a rabbit with its neck in the snare. Move at all and it will kill us. Fail to move, and we'll die just the same."

"I refuse to believe that," I whispered as we began to descend into the city. "I refuse to believe this has all been for nothing. I refuse to let it be that way. I *will* find a way to make the Empire pay and to cut this land free of their grasp. And I'll find a way to cut you free, too."

"I wish I could believe that," he breathed. "I wish you could save me. But, House Apidae, I fear our time has come. Our tragedy nears its end."

His bird twisted in the air and we sailed down in tight spirals, landing on the balcony of a fine house close to the docks. The balcony was carved to look like a swooping bird, its wings wrapping up to form railings on either side of it.

Osprey stepped from the back of his bird, still gripping me tightly. His voice was husky as he said.

"For what I do next, I hope I can be forgiven."

"Don't do anything that requires forgiveness," I said. "And then you won't have to worry."

But my heart was in my throat. I wasn't ready for torture. I hadn't had an easy life, but the regular difficulties and sacrifices of my days hadn't prepared me for actual misery and now that I knew it was coming, it was all I could do to avoid losing my breakfast.

Osprey's grip never slackened as he carried me in his strong arms. He stepped into the fine house – a place where his feather-trimmed cuffs and lace-edged handkerchiefs fit. He'd been born into this world and if he'd never Hatched, never been bound, then maybe he would have lived a soft comfortable life in a home like this one. I couldn't imagine Osprey as soft. Especially not now, with the implacable look of the executioner setting his mouth in a grim line. He wasn't even chewing a toothpick. Had he cracked them all in half?

I needed to think – needed to come up with some way to escape him, but I was just so tired. My eyes felt heavy. I reached for my bees and felt nothing.

I was going to have to kill him, wasn't I? Not Juste – well, maybe him, too – but Osprey. Because every time I came a little bit close to freedom or saw some opportunity for it, he was there, ready to drag me back into slavery. Which left me with only two choices – I either had to rescue us both or kill him so he'd stop dragging me back. And I couldn't figure out how to save him from his fate any more than he could, so that only left killing him.

I laughed so softly it was only a gust of air escaping my lips. What hubris. To think that any of that was a decision available to me when I was a captive, barely standing, supported only by his arms. But I couldn't give up. When you give up, you're worse than dead – that was the saying, right? My head was so foggy that I couldn't remember anymore.

A vision flickered over my sight – one of my bees, I realized. Far away and faint, but out there. I saw a glimpse of my brother Alect and my heart soared. He was fighting the Forbidding, carving it back with neat sword strikes, my nephew Barst on his back, strapped on with long strips of cloth the way we'd carry the little children for long hikes or walks.

The vision faded and I blinked back tears. They were still alive. They were out there – somewhere – fighting. My bee had found them. And even if I never saw them again, I could die knowing that they were safe and well. There was a strength in the thought that eclipsed everything else.

I let the hope of that fill me as Osprey led me deeper into the fine home. Whoever owned it, loved the sea. Every knickknack was a sailor's from the blown glass buoys on one of the small tables to the collection of shells displayed behind glass. Fishing spears were set in a case on one wall and a vibrant painting of a ship in sail was on another. My fingers itched to grab one of those spears, but Osprey held me close as he descended the stairs into the floor below. The strength of his arms should have been a comfort to me, but they were my cage. His footsteps seemed to drag, slower and slower as if the dread of what was to come was filling him, too.

A Claw stopped us at the foot of the stairs and Osprey answered her questions in curt, clipped words while I let my eyes roam across the sprawling entrance at the bottom of the stairs. The Claws had not been gentle to the house here. Furniture and vases were smashed. Curtains ripped from the windows. There was a double guard at the main door of the house, but there was also a blood smear across the floor leading into a room with another set of Claws guarding the door.

My limbs began to tremble. It was that blood smear. It promised things that made my insides skitter like insects across the floor. And it reminded me of the temple underground where Juste Montpetit had manifested snakes and then tried to kill me.

I gripped Osprey's arm as we passed the guard at the foot of the stairs, my strength finally failing me utterly. Osprey didn't even pause as he drew me in tighter, almost embracing me as he carried me – his arms like rock and far too strong to escape – as he followed the blood trail.

But wasn't this the way it had been all along? It had been love that had bound me to follow them to this city, love that had me save Le Majest's life, love that made me endure all of this – love of my family and the desire to see them safe and free. My love for them had taken my hand and led me into the darkness. And his love for those children was doing the same with him right now.

"Please," I whispered, knowing full well it was futile. I couldn't stop myself. I couldn't turn the instinct to survive off. It was deep in my core layers.

Osprey's jaw bulged as he clenched his teeth against my plea, a sheen of sweat coating his forehead as if he was about to face the Emperor's Vultures. "Don't beg, Apidae. Spare me that."

The door swung open and the guards stepped aside as Osprey

carried me into a wide gallery. It must have been used for parties or dinners. The walls were paneled and painted white, small pillars rose at intervals along them – also white – bearing marble carvings of albatrosses. This must be House Albatross. A fitting thing. Even I, raised far from the sea, had heard of the way sailors viewed those birds – a sign of both luck and disaster. Zayana and her love of signs would be thrilled by this.

At the center of the room, Juste Montpetit stood, staring at the toe of his boot as a translucent snake slithered around his shoulders and twisted across his forehead like a crown. He looked up as we entered, his huge brown eyes brightening as they met mine in what could only be described as hunger.

CHAPTER TWENTY-TWO

My stomach flipped and – foolishly, knowing better – I clung to Osprey like a frightened child.

The gallery was so full of people that I couldn't hope to identify them all. I caught sight of Butiez and Xectare in one corner pouring over maps on a table. What had Wing Xectare said to Le Majest to return to his favor? I would have thought that he'd never forgive her for leaving him on the battlefield when he needed her blood to save him. Claws guarded every window their postures stiff and expressions tense. A man with a nautical look to him – who I assumed owned the house – was sitting in a corner with a woman who might be his wife. Both of them looked frightened and unhappy, but they kept their eyes to the floor as I surveyed the room. I'd get no help from them. There were clusters of Claws and whispering huddles of people who looked like High'uns. The High'uns were dressed in their best Imperial style, long flowing court robes on the women and tight trousers ending in heavily embroidered short jackets on the men. The women wore their hair in intricate braided caps and the men wore theirs in short tails at the backs of their necks and the whole thing had the effect of a dinner party gone horribly wrong. They were gathered around the room like murders of ravens, here to feast on death.

"Look around," Le Majest said in a deceptively light tone.

"This room, and everyone in it, is mine. Do you see that?"

I said nothing. I wasn't going to play his games. I stared defiantly into his eyes, showing him with my gaze that I refused to be broken.

His face grew tight. "Put her down."

Osprey set my feet on the floor wordlessly, but I could feel his heart pounding in his chest. I could feel the tension in his muscles as he supported my swaying weight beside him with one powerful arm. He pulled a toothpick out from his sleeve and jammed it between his teeth. It snapped and he fumbled for another one, his hand shaking.

"Can she not stand alone? She struck me as someone who always wants to." Juste Montpetit hadn't moved, and yet it felt like his voice was sliding toward me slowly, like a snake prowling.

Osprey pulled his arm away and I barely kept my feet under me. It took all my concentration to remain standing. My legs felt like jelly and my head swam.

Come on, Aella. Don't let them see you fall.

"Those bees have taken a toll on you, it would seem," Juste Montpetit said, and his words almost sounded sympathetic until he crossed to me with a single step, seized my hair in his fist and shook me, his voice still a whisper, a mad glitter in his eye. "And what toll did you make me pay? You took away those bees and left me in agony. Worse – you've left your mark on me, girl. That honeycomb can't be removed or I will die. That's what the healer said. And kept saying even after I gave her many reasons to stop saying it."

My eyes followed the trail of blood across the gallery floor to where it ended in a slumped pile beside the owners of the house.

That couldn't be the healer … could it?

Juste Montpetit followed my eyes and smiled.

"That's right. Look at her and think about how that could be you. You defied me. You ran from me. You took away your bees but still left your curse in my belly. You marked me with your magic and I am marked by no one."

"You seem fine now," I said through lips thick with exhaustion.

"As in well? Whole?" he asked, adjusting his grip to turn me so I had to look at him.

He shoved me down to my knees, fist still tight in my hair. It brought my eyes level with his belt and with the spot where his torn, blood-stained shirt still parted and the angry red flesh of his belly parted, too, revealing the glowing honeycomb holding him together, a salve around it.

He meant me to see that, I realized. But what I was unable to stop staring at was the dagger in his belt – a new one with an albatross inlaid on the hilt. Good luck or disaster. It could be either – or both. It was almost within reach, if I was mad enough to take the chance. I licked my lips, trying to judge if I was fast enough to take it and make the kill before Osprey ran me through with his sword.

I would be able to do it this time. It wouldn't feel like murder. It would feel like the end of a nightmare.

"I've been trying to decide how to repay you for this," Juste said silkily. He dropped my hair so suddenly that I sagged as he stepped back. I'd lost my chance to grab the dagger. "It ties me to you. Did you know that? That's the only interesting bit of information that healer was able to give me – that the honeycomb ties me to you. If you die, it's gone. Which means I don't want you to die."

I looked up, meeting his eyes. He didn't want to kill me? My heart stuttered on the burst of hope.

His smile twisted cruelly. "Don't mistake that for mercy. I don't want you dead, but that doesn't mean I don't plan to punish you." He snapped his fingers. "Osprey."

Osprey didn't move and Juste Montpetit's eyes narrowed. "Did you think that was a suggestion? Have you forgotten that you have to obey me? And if you don't hit her when I say strike, you'll feel that flash of agony that tells you one of your little souls has been whisked away. What's more precious to you, Guardian? Your charges' lives or this girl's pretty face?"

I heard Osprey's toothpick snap for a second time. And then, lightning fast, he had a dagger in his hand. Juste's head cocked to the side, eyes narrowing and I felt my own eyes grow large. Did he plan to stab me with it.

Osprey's throat bobbed as he visibly swallowed and then he plunged the dagger into his other hand. Juste bit back a snarl, clutching his hand to his chest as Osprey removed the dagger, letting his blood spill onto the floor.

"I'm ordering you, " Juste hissed. "You will –"

His words cut off as the dagger plunged again – this time into Osprey's left thigh. He stumbled at the blow, Le Majest mirroring him exactly. Both of them clenched their jaws against the pain and then a light of malevolence filled Juste's eye and he pulled himself to his feet.

"In the mood for games, *guardian*? I can play games. I'm very good at them." He snapped his fingers and two Claws stepped forward. He waved a vague hand at me. "The eye, if you please."

Before I could gasp they stepped forward and a fist crashed into my face.

I sprawled across the floor, head ringing, pain flashing through my body. I didn't remember hitting the ground, didn't remember the strike. I tried to twist to get my hands under me but my vision was blurred. I reached up gently and felt my right eye already swelling.

"Do I need to order my Claws to stop you, guardian?" Juste asked in a tight voice. I could see he was clutching one arm. Osprey must have stabbed himself again.

"If you must. I will not stop until you do." Osprey's voice was equally tight. "There's no need to keep torturing her."

Le Majest snorted. I didn't understand why he wasn't ordering his Claws to stop Osprey. This dance between them was opaque to me.

"There is now," he said viciously. His voice turned to me. "Up. On your knees."

I moaned.

"Or would you rather I have them kick you in the belly – right where you put your mark in me? You may not be able to stand for a week when their finished."

I gasped, pulling myself to my knees and swaying there.

"See?" Montpetit asked. "Is obedience so difficult?

Osprey stood behind him, his bird gone and his eyes dark with shame. I tried to meet them, but he kept his gaze from me, darting away whenever I tried to catch it. His cheeks were hot just like the blood spilling now from hand and leg and side.

He was doing that for me. To try to stop my torture or at least keep himself from being the one to do it to me. It was … heartbreakingly noble … and yet even that defiance was not enough.

Le Majest would not be stopped by pain. His cruelty burned too bright for that. I turned back to meet his eyes again.

"You're having me beaten?" I asked in a mild tone, feigning surprise. "After I saved your city?"

"*My* city?" Juste Montpetit asked, his snake rolling off his head to creep, twisting round and round his arm until the head curled up from the tips of his fingers, arching into an S shape and flicking its tongue through the air. Around us, his gathered court gasped with shocked delight as if he'd just brought a twisted party trick to the ruined ball. "Well, that's progress. You've admitted that something is mine. Does that mean that you realize that you are mine, too?"

"Le Majest?" there was a cough from in the room and he spun, poison in his eyes. I followed his gaze to see Claw Brielle there, surrounded by other Claws. They shifted uneasily as she spoke. "If you please, Le Majest, the Hatchling speaks the truth about the city. Lord Captain Claw Afalai has stated that the flag communications saved us. Without them, we were too unprepared to form an effective defense."

She shouldn't have said that. She shouldn't have done that. Even if I hadn't known that myself, I would know it in the way Osprey's eyes clouded in pain. They were hooded like the eyes of an eagle.

"We speak only the truth in the Winged Empire," Le Majest said mildly, watching Claw Brielle with a gentle smile.

"As you say, Le Majest," she said boldly.

"Take this Claw and escort her out of the city. Take her armor and weaponry. She is banished from our Empire. If she does not love the truth, she has no place among us."

"Le Majest?" Brielle gasped, eyes wide. She was already being dragged away by her fellow Claws.

"Oh, and take her tongue. We speak only the truth in the Winged Empire," Juste Montpetit repeated, his eyes glittering with madness. "You're writing the truth right now, aren't you, Butiez?"

"As you say, Le Majest," Butiez called from his corner of the room. "I am preparing a request for four full companies of Claws with Tern ships to accommodate them for the security of this colony to be led by our gracious crown prince whose presence has already banished the enemy from this city and is required to make this entire continent secure."

"Carry on," Juste hissed, his spirit snake hissing with him. "See? It is not a girl with bees who has saved this city – or will save this city and *all* of Far Stones – it is the crown prince. I plan to make this continent safe again."

He said 'safe' with a smooth tone as if it was a threat – which of course it was. 'Safe' only meant under his control. 'Safe' only ever meant owned.

I felt the swell of my eye and thought of him beating all of us into the ground, of cutting out tongues and eyes. Of taking our weapons and our ability to speak the truth – the real truth, not his 'truth.' My jaw hardened and my bees began to buzz in my head again. I grasped at their buzz, desperate for the feel of their power.

Montpetit nodded to his Claws. "The belly this time."

And before I could flinch, pain burst through me, stealing my vision for a moment, leaving me curled over my agonized insides, heaving, gasping for breath. My thoughts swirled out of my head, leaving nothing but pain and gasps of air. Pain and more pain. I thought I felt another blow and another, but I was nothing but pain drifting on pain and more pain.

My head cleared enough to pull myself onto all fours and dry heave. There was nothing left in my belly. I'd lost it all a long time ago.

"Enough, Osprey!" Juste snarled, his voice raw. "Forbidding take it!"

Rough hands pulled me back to my knees.

"You might be wondering why I am having you beaten before me," Juste Montpetit swam in my vision as if he was underwater and I was looking down at him. His face had a drawn look, despite his triumph, as if he was fighting as much pain as I was, and his words came out tight as if he had to force his tongue to speak.

I sucked in a long, agonized breath.

"I assumed it was because you were too weak to do it yourself," I gasped. If I was going to die. I would die with defiance on my tongue.

He moved like a lightning strike, grabbing my throat in his hand and pulling me up to my feet. Agony shot through me. He leaned in so close I could smell his breath, whispering now.

"The people of this land gave you something. Something that was meant for me."

"Something you were too cowardly to take for yourself," I whispered, barely able to speak at all through my crushed throat.

He hissed – just that, a hiss like a snake.

"Something that I don't dare lose. And yet, I want you to see that rebellion is useless. That it will only get you pain and misery. Everyone who speaks for you – even in a small way – will be removed. Sentenced to die wandering outside the walls. Anyone who moves to protect you will be tortured to death. But you – you will stay by my side and you will serve me. I've realized where I've heard of bees before. There's a poem about them.

"The bees drive back the rest,

The bells of freedom ring,

They conquer and they best

Cute, don't you think?"

I didn't respond and he squeezed harder, the snake unfurling from his hand and wrapping itself with silky cold around my neck and mouth.

"It means that you're part of this – your bees are required. And they will serve me as I conquer the world."

I gasped in a breath as he relaxed his grip enough to let me speak. I shivered at the feeling of the snake sliding around my neck. "I thought the Winged Empire already owned the world. What do you need to conquer?"

"Everything," he whispered in my ear. "And you will be there to watch it all. It turns out I need both those bees and the gift that my new allies left in that pretty head of yours."

"Allies? They just attacked your city."

"And wasn't that perfectly timed?" he whispered in my ear. "Because how can my father deny me troops to put down their forces when they've attacked one of our cities? And as they melt into that tangle you call the Forbidding, I will be stealing my father's army from under his nose and establishing my hold in this rocky misery of a land. But it is only a starting point. Only a beginning. From here, we will take over the Winged Empire and you will help me conquer. I will dress you in silks and you will call forth your bees and you will smile beside me as I rule the world."

"And why will I do that?" I asked.

"Because after I have Osprey carve my mark into you, I am going to marry you," he whispered. "How kind of me to show you such mercy? Don't you think? How gracious of me to bind myself in matrimony to the land I defend and the people I rule."

I gagged, not just because the snake was wrapped around my neck. Not just because of his words in my ear, but because now he trailed his lips across my cheek and kissed me – chastely, cruelly, tauntingly – on my lips.

CHAPTER TWENTY-THREE

His snake released me and I collapsed to the ground, my hands around my throat clutching the ache there, my knees watery and weak at the thought of being bound to him forever – not just as a slave or property, but as a wife. I felt so ill that my other injuries seemed to fade in comparison as cold sweat slicked my forehead and spine and I began to shake, nausea rolling over me in queasy waves.

Don't give up, Aella, don't give up.

There was still time to do something about this.

I swallowed down bile and forced myself to shaky knees.

"Take her upstairs, Osprey, and strip off those bloody clothes," Juste smirked and there was something cruel in the look he turned on Osprey. His eyes narrowed like he knew a secret. "Take this knife. You've already bloodied your own." He handed Osprey the albatross knife. "Carve an image of my snake into that strong back of hers and mark her as mine with your own hand. And when you're finished, you will dress her in one of the silks in those fancy closets that Madame Jesuie keeps. They're close in size. I'll marry her as soon as I can find a Skybinder. There has to be one around here somewhere."

"Marry, Le Majest?" Osprey's voice seemed to stumble.

"Well, what did you think all this was about, Guardian? I don't take this kind of time for just anyone. I have affairs of state waiting for me. You – of all people – should know how precious my life is and how valuable my time. After all, you went to great lengths to save me."

His smirk seemed to mock us both.

My breath hitched, choking in my throat worse than it had when the snake was wrapped around me. The thought of his slimy hands all over me – of no barriers between us – rippled through me like the Forbidding. I wanted to sink into unconsciousness. I wanted to run. I wanted someone to save me.

But no one was going to save me.

I bit my lip. I could lunge now and try to take the dagger he'd given Osprey, but I knew Osprey was fast and the room was full of Le Majest's allies. They'd take the knife from me before I could stab their precious crown prince. But Osprey was going to drag me away from here in a minute. We'd be alone. That would be my chance. He was already weakened, bleeding in a half a dozen places from wounds he'd inflicted on himself – wounds that had probably saved me from a worse beating.

I bit the inside of my cheek, trying to stay calm, trying to be patient. Hot, tangy blood seeped into my mouth.

"Stop gawking and obey, Osprey," Juste Montpetit said, looking once over his shoulder as he turned to Counsellor Butiez. I followed his gaze, surprised to see Osprey glaring at Juste, fists clenched at his side. Behind him, his bird blinked in and out of existence as if it was bursting free with every beat of his heart. He trembled and as he shook, the bright glow in his chest shone right through his shirt and jacket as if it was somehow heating up or under pressure. Juste's smile grew at the sight. He looked just like a child who'd been given an extra treat. "Or did you want the consequences of disobedience? That can be arranged."

Osprey made a quick sign of the bird and grabbed my arm, pulling me to my feet. Everything hurt. I stumbled, fighting against waves of pain as I tried to find my feet.

Osprey cursed quietly, trying to support me, but I was as wobbly as a fresh-born fawn and his hands were slicked with his own blood.

It all came down to this. I'd been debating all this time about whether I could save him or whether I would have to kill him to be free. In a few minutes, we would be out of sight and it would be easy enough to pretend I'd lost my balance and lean into him for support. I would take the dagger then. But could I wound him enough to stop him from chasing me as I fled? Any hesitation and I would certainly lose. He was faster and stronger than I was and had training. I would have to be certain of what I was going to do because I would only have surprise on my side.

I tried to slow my racing heartbeat. It wasn't helping me think clearly. Not when every muscle in my body was screaming at me not to hurt Osprey – especially now, after he gave himself all those wounds to try to protect me. I had to ignore that instinct. I had no other option.

We exited into the entranceway outside the gallery and I slipped, falling hard to the floor. My body was not cooperating, and my right eye had swollen shut. I bit my lip. How was I going to steal the dagger and do *anything* in this state?

Strong hands reached down, lifting me up and into his embrace. He slung one arm under my knees and the other under my back, pulling me to his chest like a small child.

"Os – "

He cut me off with a sharp shake of his head and began to whistle as he carried me slowly through the entrance and to the wide staircase, leaving a trail of blood droplets behind him. It was the song he'd sung me when Juste had offered me as a substitute to the snakes. A song low and haunting, sad and mysterious. I sank into it, my heart crying silently with the low lullaby.

It shouldn't have come to this. But it was always coming to this, from the moment he plucked me from my hatching. It was always going to be me plunging a dagger into his heart or him killing me under orders from Le Majest.

My left eye was blurry. I reached up to wipe it and realized it was glazed with a single, unshed tear. My eye met his desperate gaze for just a moment as his whistle intensified and his cheeks burned hot. Neither of us wanted this. Neither of us liked who we were in this moment. Could I really stick a knife into a man who looked at me like this? With tenderness and a breaking heart?

He clung to me as he carried me, as if I was his anchor to sanity as much as his intended victim and I began to build my resolve. He was trapped in an endless cycle of villainy to save these children under his care, but I would never be free as long as he had me within his grasp. And while they would die with his suicide, they would not die with him if it was at the hand of another. I'd be saving him with this. And judging by what he had done to himself down there, he might even welcome this.

His song faltered as we reached the top of the stairs and left the guards behind.

"Hold on, House Apidae. Hold on," he whispered, carrying me down the hall and into the room we'd flown in from. The window to the balcony was still open and a light breeze stirred the filmy curtains. The smell of flowers – lavender, I thought –

filled the air. "It will be okay."

I didn't answer. I wanted the comfort – but I knew it was false. Because in a moment, he'd be trying to rip away my clothing and carve a snake into my flesh so he could present me to Juste Montpetit as a tattered bride. He might hate what he did, but he would do it all the same.

I should be silent. I shouldn't tip my hand.

I couldn't help myself.

"What were you thinking, stabbing yourself like that?"

"He feels what I feel. He hurts when I hurt."

"And do you want to make him hurt?"

"I want to make him stop. And that was the only way I could think of to do it. The only way I could keep him from destroying you and from forcing me to be the one to do it. I'm sorry – if I could have stopped it, I would have." His cheeks flushed with shame and a shudder ran through him. "I need saving as badly as you do, House Apidae. We are both pawns in this game of War and Wings."

"But I'm only a pawn because you dragged me into it. I could have run with my family. I could have killed Le Majest and fled that cathedral under the ground. But who was it who stopped me? Who kept threatening me? Who made me make a vow to him? That was you." I was trying to be gentle, but he needed to understand why I was going to do what I would do next. "You are more my captor than the crown prince will ever be, even when he marries me and forces himself on me, and tortures me day after day for the rest of my life because it will be you who keeps me there."

He stumbled, leaning hard against the wall, but still not

dropping me. He left a smear of blood against the wall. It was dripping into small pools at his feet.

"Not if I can help it. I will cut myself a hundred times to prevent it. I will –" but here his voice broke as if he didn't know what to promise.

"You're the rope binding my wrists and the knife at my throat," I whispered.

"I don't know what to do to stop it," he said, shuddering. "I'm sorry. I'm so sorry for all of it."

He set me down on my feet, but he kept going, falling to his knees. I fell to mine, too, but only because I barely had the strength to stand.

He blinked rapidly, fighting his emotions, his face twisting bitterly. It made him look younger than he was, like a child. How could I save him from his binding and from himself? Perhaps death would be a mercy. Or perhaps, like him, I was just making excuses for myself.

"I'm sorry, too," I said biting my lip.

He leaned in, bringing a hand up to cup my face, his eyes filled with tender agony.

"You break me, House Apidae, and burn my soul to the ground. You salt its fields and leave it weeping."

I breathed in a long breath as he spoke, letting the hum of the bees fill me with certainty. I reached for his belt, snatched up the dagger and jabbed it into his chest.

He looked down at me with shock, snatching his hand from my face. But he didn't stop me.

Os flared to life behind him, hovering there but not attacking.

"He never thought to order me to defend myself," he whispered. "He didn't think I would ever meet my match."

But I wasn't done yet. I hadn't stabbed him very deeply. And that was for a reason.

Ruthlessly, I reached out and grabbed his jacket, tearing it and the shirt beneath, to expose his muscular chest. His skin shone with the sweat of stress and fear. I had hit my mark. The dagger pierced the skin where the feather glowed under it.

"I'm at your mercy," he said, eyes meeting mine. His eyes sparkled slightly with the gleam of unshed tears as his arms parted, baring himself to me.

I swallowed, overwhelmed by the trust and vulnerability.

I wrenched the dagger out with little effort. It had sliced through the top layer of skin and muscle, deeper than I'd hoped, but with any luck, not too deep … not lethally deep.

"Do as you must," he breathed.

I shifted my grip around the handle of the dagger, took a deep breath, and pierced his skin again in a quick motion, like killing a chicken – fast and as efficient as possible to spare the victim. I sliced his skin and muscle, worrying the knife in under that glowing feather and then prying one end of it free. It reached out like the tangle of the Forbidding, reaching toward me as if it could grasp me and pull me in. I caught it between my fingers and tried to pull.

He made a soft keening sound and I looked up to see his teeth gritted in agony.

None of this would matter if I didn't finish the job. I wanted to save him, not to kill him. I wanted to save us both.

I planted a foot on his hip for leverage, grabbed the feather in both hands, and pulled for all I was worth.

A wail of pain escaped his lips and I heard warning cries below.

"Forbidding take it!" I swore, sawing off the end of the feather that was free. Half gone. It was half gone.

Footsteps pounded up the stairs – multiple feet. I had seconds.

Osprey swayed, his teeth still clenched, blood pouring from his ruined chest. He grabbed my wrist with one hand and looked into my eyes.

"A valiant attempt, House Apidae."

He collapsed to the ground at the same time that the first guard dashed into the room.

I spun and ran for the balcony, begging my bees, "Please! Please, come! Please!"

My heart wrenched at leaving Osprey like that, but I had no choice. This was my one chance. My one hope of escape.

I ran to the edge of the balcony, climbing up the carved wing.

"My hope is in you," I breathed, like a prayer … and leapt.

CHAPTER TWENTY-FOUR

Bees poured from my mouth and hands, speeding so fast that they stung my skin as they passed. They formed below me, slowing my descent as I dropped through the air. Humming a music that resonated deep within me, they bore me to the cobbles below like a gentle cloud. I reached out my hands and let them pour through my fingers like rain.

I'd done it. I was free.

I wobbled as I caught myself on the cobbles, wavering for a moment as my bees disappeared. They left me breathless and sagging. That one, sudden burst had taken every bit of strength I had left in me. One solitary bee buzzed around my head.

"Hold on little buddy," I whispered to him. "I need you yet."

I forced myself to stand, wavering as my legs protested. I needed to move. Now. Before I was discovered. But where? The docks were close. I'd flee there.

I ran, making it only three staggering steps before something snagged my foot and I tripped, falling heavily to the cobbled ground. I grunted in pain as the fall flared through all my injuries.

But it wasn't a simple trip. Something had my foot. I kicked out at it, but I was being dragged across the cobbles and I couldn't twist enough to see what had me in its grasp. My injured face and belly bumped across the rough edges of the stones and it was all I could do to hunch myself and protect my injuries.

My head hit something, and stars danced across my vision as I came to a stop.

I blinked my one good eye open, gasping with pain.

Inches from my face was the face of Le Majest.

"It seems you have overcome my guardian," he said smoothly, his wide eyes far from innocent in how they looked me up and down. "We won't make that mistake again. Will we?"

He flicked his finger and I stood up – not intentionally, but something stood me up. Something that was wrapped all around me, squeezing me. It pulled me along, upright behind him as he walked back into Sunset House. His fist was clenched tightly to his chest.

I tried to struggle, but I couldn't find any kind of purchase against the bonds of the spirit snake, and my strength was spent in using the bees to break my fall. I could barely hold my head up. It lolled against my chest.

"Flee," I whispered to my bee. "Find help. Or just get away."

It darted away but I was so weak that I couldn't even tell where it had gone.

"Guard the door. Keep everyone out," Le Majest ordered as he led the snake holding me into another room of the house. "And find a healer for the guardian. His wounds irritate me."

Osprey had survived the botched feather removal. I hadn't killed him by accident. But I hadn't saved him either – not with the desperate feather gamble and not by taking his life.

Juste led me into a room that had once been a study. Maybe it still was. Whoever had owned it must have studied strange things. There were books on shelves, a desk, a bird totem – albatross – and a fireplace, but that was where the normality of the room ended. One of the walls – a thick stone wall – had manacles and chains across it. Small bottles and metal instruments lined the wall.

"Looks like the kind of place you'd expect from one of my Vultures, doesn't it?" Juste's mild tone made my skin crawl. "That's what I thought when I saw it. A place for torture and confessions. But, apparently, the owner of this home was studying your beloved Forbidding. He would cut a piece of it – living – from the countryside, bind it with chains and bring it back here to study. He had no success, but that only seemed to drive him harder. He's an inspiration to me, you know. I don't like giving up on things easily, either."

His snake pulled me against the wall and Juste strolled over, grabbing the clanking manacles and strapping me in place with them before his snake pulled away from me.

"If you expect me to confess something, I have nothing to confess," I said thickly.

"I don't expect you to confess anything," Juste Montpetit said sweetly. "That's not the point of this little demonstration. No, this is to teach you two things. First, that your resistance – while good for the genetics of any children you might bear me – is useless against me and a waste of our time. I can't have you stabbing my Wings left and right, can I? That's hardly the type of behavior we want to see in the peaceful society I am preaching."

"You aren't bringing peace here. You brought that snake attack," I said. I felt so weak that even talking was difficult. I slumped in the manacles, wishing I could sit or lay on the study floor. They were attached to both hands and feet, keeping me spread-eagled uncomfortably.

"Of course I did," he said gently, as if speaking to a small child. "You get what you ask for in life, property. And I am asking for everything. The whole Empire and everything in it."

"Won't you get that when your father dies?"

"In fifty or a hundred years?" he asked, sneering. "We're long-lived in the Imperial family. My father has songbird Wings who sing to him every day, increasing his long life and energy. I'll be an old man before he dies and by then he'll have wasted all our resources on his endless conquests. I have other plans for the Empire. Plans that won't wait. I wouldn't tell you about them – but as my wife, you'll need to know because you will be helping me to promote them."

"And you're not afraid that I'll tell?" I asked.

"Not at all," he said with a smile. "Especially since I'm going to take your tongue in a moment. You use it so poorly that it's sure to be an improvement."

I gasped.

"Don't worry, you'll still be able to gasp in horror. Just like that."

I swallowed, my mouth suddenly dry. If I hadn't attacked Osprey …

"And now you're thinking that if you'd only let Osprey give you my mark and dress you in silk we wouldn't have to do this. And you're right," he said, smiling gently. "So, remember this the next time you defy me. It doesn't have to go poorly for you – if you remember that you are mine. That you belong to me. That I will do to you as I please. Apparently, threatening that bedraggled family of yours does nothing. Killing them before you does nothing. Ordering the only person who tried to protect you to mark you for me does nothing – oh, did you think I didn't see that my guardian had a soft spot for you? I'm not a fool, property. Or should I call you wife? You will be that very soon. My Claws are getting me a Skysinger to make it so."

"You're hurting yourself as much as me by marrying me," I said defiantly.

"Do you think so?" he asked, tilting his head as if he was really considering my words. His fist was still clasped to his chest as if he was trying to hold something in it. "The healer says I'm bound to you. I need your honeycomb and it vanishes if you're dead. And my snake allies warned me that the gifts they gave you are necessary for me. I need to keep you close. And what is closer than a wife?"

"And the second reason?" I asked.

"What?"

"You said this was to teach me two things. The first was that my resistance was useless."

He smiled. "At least you listen. You can put your ears to good use when I take your tongue. But yes, there was another reason. It's to teach you once and for all that you are mine – in every way. I own your every action, every thought, every murmur. I own you, body and soul, and you shall never be free of me."

I shivered as his face went blank suddenly and he lifted a hand and his snake returned, slithering from his palm and swaying side to side almost as if it were dancing. The movement was hypnotizing. I tried to fight it.

"Please," I begged my bees. "Please."

But I couldn't feel them – not even their buzz. I was too tired for magic. I was too tired to do anything at all.

Except for maybe some last defiance while I still had a tongue. "May what you do here today ring condemnation through the years of your life. May it sour days of sunshine and dash comfort to the floor. May all love cast you out in this life and the next."

His eyes narrowed, but it was the only sign that he'd heard me at all. He reached out and caressed the snake. It slid up his arm, twisting around his torso and face lovingly as he whispered softly to it. As he spoke, it glowed a brighter green and began to swell. He must be very good at invoking to have come so far in just a few days. His snake had grown, and it seemed more vicious than ever.

It flowed down his other arm and to the ground as he continued his long, steady whispered chant. I couldn't make out the words, but somehow I didn't have to. I could feel them – ambition and cruelty, possessiveness and power. They twisted through his chant like strands of poison.

His eyes glazed over and his lips parted with pleasure as he kept whispering his steady stream to the glowing adder. It rippled across the ground, slowly sliding toward me.

I backed up into the stone wall behind me, my manacles clanking as they hit it. But there was nowhere to go. I was exposed and at his mercy.

"If you have any tricks," I whispered. "Now is the time."

My little bee buzzed, creeping down the manacle. But it was only one bee. It was not enough to save me. I barely had the power to lift my head. I certainly didn't have the power to call on bees.

The snake tangled around my leg and I gasped in horror as it wrapped around my ankle and slid up my leg. I couldn't help the cry of terror that escaped my lips or the terror that shuddered through me when Juste smiled at my fear. His beautiful mouth curved into an expression that might inspire Imperial painters. He loved this – my every flinch, my every cry.

I fought my own body, trying to remain still – trying not to give him the satisfaction as the snake wrapped around my belly and began to slide higher yet. I trembled under it as it wove and danced over my skin.

A sense of wrongness filled me, making me feel like a trespasser in my own body, but as though my soul been trespassed *on*.

And then his spirit snake was plunging through my body, disappearing into me. Pain ripped through every nerve of my body as it darted its adder head into my chest. Hot spikes of pain shoved through my chest. I screamed, throwing my head back, unable to control my reaction now.

Surely, there must be something I could call on for help.

But I was alone. I was at the end of myself. I had nothing left to give except my desperation and fear.

I focused on my bees, but there was only that single bee, working its way into the lock on my manacle. A valiant attempt … but even if my magic succeeded there, it would only free one hand. Still, I spoke to the bee with my mind, Keep going! Free me!

The snake removed its head and began to slither up around my collar bone, tongue flickering in the air.

"I would guess that you considered yourself special when

you manifested bees," Juste said speculatively. "They do have some interesting properties. Such as healing. I won't deny that it has been personally helpful to me that they exist – even if I wouldn't have needed them had you not stabbed me in the belly in the first place. But they aren't much of a weapon. More of a distraction. You wouldn't believe the thrill I get from this snake. The pain it can manifest. The way it can violate the natural bounds of physical and spiritual – it was like meeting my inner self for the very first time. It's powerful and beautiful and deadly – everything I've ever wanted to be.

"And when I am not with you, wife, I will leave my snake with you to remind you of how you are mine. But that will be rare, for I shall keep me with you always. What could be more intimate than the bond shared between husband and wife, unless it is the bond shared by us as my manifestation has free range through you, rummaging through your spirit and plundering it as it wishes? Do you think snakes eat bees? I think mine would like to try.

"I shall enjoy being wed to you. When I am free from affairs of state, I can watch your reaction to my magic, watch your eyes grow wide in horror, and listen to your wordless screams whenever I need reminding that I truly am as powerful as I need to be."

The snake reared up, swaying in front of my eyes. I kept my jaw locked, my mouth firmly closed. Juste's grin grew larger. He knew my closed mouth was no barrier to the snake.

"No last words for me?" he teased.

I tensed, pulling at the manacles. One clicked open, dropping as it freed my right hand. I grabbed at the snake and my hand passed right through it as my bee buzzed past my face.

A laugh burst from Juste – high-pitched and rusty – like he wasn't used to laughing.

"I like you better when you're fighting it."

Something banged on the door and he glanced toward it, his hand lifting to cup his injured belly. If only my bees were still there to draw on. Their honeycomb was still there. I could feel it even when my eyes were closed or I was out of the room.

Wait. I could feel it.

Why would that be?

There was a burst of red light from outside the small study window and more banging on the door. Juste cursed under his breath, glancing from me to the door and back. He gasped, his hand flying up to grip one of his shoulders as he grimaced in pain.

"Someone wants to interrupt our fun. We'll have to be quick."

His snake hissed, twisting back and forth as if deciding how to dart through my closed teeth and rip my tongue from my mouth. My eye glazed with tears as I tried to keep it in sight.

A muffled shout and more banging on the other side made Juste clench his jaw and his fist. I was running out of time.

I felt the manacle on my right foot fall loose and the second it did, I *pulled* with all my mental strength at the honeycomb in his belly. What had been given, could be taken back. Energy flowed from it to me, filling me up, replacing what I'd lost.

The snake disappeared. Juste's jaw dropped open.

A second manacle fell from my other foot and bees swarmed from my hands, filling the room with their buzz and filling my heart with joy.

Juste stumbled to one knee, hatred flashing in his eyes as he fought to stay upright, just like I had moments before. The banging on the door stopped abruptly as my last manacle fell and I raced for the window, fumbling for the lock and shoving it open.

“Wherever you go, I will find you,” Juste whispered from where he leaned on all fours, trying to keep himself from collapsing. “This is not over.”

One of my bees zipped out of my hand, circling his head. I left it there.

“Of course it isn’t,” I agreed as I shoved through the window. “It’s only just begun.”

CHAPTER TWENTY-FIVE

I leapt out into the street toward the light of the red bird frantically flapping in front of me. Ignoring the shouts behind me, I sprinted after it and down an alley. The energy I'd stolen from Juste was buoying me up, making my agony fade away temporarily.

The red bird flew ahead of me, as frantic as I was, dashing down a street and plunging down a second alley, leading me to an open door. My bees began to fade as my stolen energy sapped away. My magic trickled down to a single bee. I'd lost my hold on them. I was beginning to lose the strength in my legs, too.

Don't give out on me now!

The red bird fluttered, agitated and I hurried after it, through a narrow door and down into the earth and the darkness. Hopefully, Zayana was in there somewhere. Hopefully, I could trust her in a world where everyone seemed to want something from me.

We were in a cellar where the barrels lined up like soldiers.

The bird slowed and I followed carefully into a narrow passage that dove deeper still into the ground. My pain was returning as my strength faded. I doubled over, clutching my damaged belly, my head ringing with the reminder that I'd been hit in the face with Osprey's powerful fist. The pain was worse after those few minutes without it – as if I was being struck all over again.

The passage widened into an open door, the sound of lapping water on the other side. My legs were heavy as rocks as I stumbled through the door and collapsed as I passed through it into warm arms.

"I've got you, Aella," Zayana murmured. "We've got you."

My last bee faded out.

"Quick," I heard Ivo whisper. "Get her into the boat. They're in the passage. We don't have much time."

She helped me into a small boat tied up in a man-made channel. I slumped in the bow, resting my head along the rail of the boat. It was the same little fishing boat we'd arrived in, I realized.

My escape seemed to have cost every last scrap of my energy. I could barely lift my head.

"What's wrong with her?" Zayana asked as she shoved the skiff off the dock and leapt in.

"Drained," Ivo said shortly. "She used up all her energy escaping. Did Flame see how she got out?"

"I don't know! I can't see through his eyes yet!"

"Don't panic. You did very well." Ivo's voice was strained and they both faded into grunts of effort as they turned to rowing. "Harpy would have been too noticeable but Flame is the perfect size for a stealth maneuver like that one."

Water lapped against the boat as it slid quietly into the dark channel. I fought my heavy eyelid, sinking into the hard side of the boat as relief – like a fire burning the Forbidding – rolled across my heart.

I had escaped. My tongue wouldn't be removed today. I wouldn't be marrying Juste or doomed to have his snake violate my body at will.

"Throw the tarp over her," Ivo whispered and a canvas that smelled of mildew was draped over me.

Minutes – or maybe hours, I was losing track – passed and then there was a murmur of voices over the tarp.

The boat kept moving and once again I was escaping out onto the water. Only this time, it heaved and rolled with the tide. I lifted the edge of the tarp and caught a glimpse of the city, lit with lanterns and torches.

Over everything else in the dark sky, a purplish-white Osprey shot up into the sky like an arrow, bursting open as its wings unfurled and it fell into a swoop, circling over the city.

I put my hand over the cuff at my wrist. The feather within was growing cooler by the second.

I let the tarp fall back over me.

Everything faded as my consciousness fled with my strength.

BEHIND THE SCENES:

USA Today bestselling author, Sarah K. L. Wilson loves spinning a yarn and if it paints a magical new world, twists something old into something reborn, or makes your heart pound with excitement ... all the better. Sarah hails from the rocky Canadian Shield in Northern Ontario – learning patience and tenacity from the long months of icy cold – where she lives with her husband and two small boys. You might find her building fires in her woodstove and wishing she had a dragon handy to light them for her

Sarah would like to thank Barbara, Melissa and Eugenia for their incredible work in beta reading and proofreading this book. Without their big hearts and passion for stories, this book would not be the same.

Sarah has the deepest regard for the talent of her phenomenal artist Luciano Fleitas who created the gorgeous cover art that accompanies this book. Without his work, it would be so much harder to show off this story the way it deserves. She also wants to thank her editor, Melissa, who tried her best to make this book better. Any errors remaining are all Sarah's.

Thanks also to the Noble Order of Female Fantasy Authors who keep me sane – sort of. And for my beloved husband, Cale and sons Neville and Leif who are endlessly patient as I talk to them about bookish passions.

Reviews are always welcome! If you liked this book, please tell someone!

Visit my website for more information:

www.sarahklwilson.com

Lightning Source UK Ltd.
Milton Keynes UK
UKHW022210011020
370885UK00010B/274/J